A Candlelight Ecstasy Romance ®

**HOW SHE HAD ACHED FOR THE SEARING HEAT
OF HIS DESIRE—DESIRE THAT AROUSED HER
TO INTOLERABLE HEIGHTS. . . .**

As he lightly kissed her eyelids, the contours of her high cheekbones, the sensitized scented hollows beneath her ears, she knew
she was a fool to succumb, but she was unable to push him away.
She made a soft sound that was almost a whimper and heard his
low triumphant laugh, but all that mattered at that moment was
his kiss. She responded with an ardor that erupted from the
innermost core of her being. Her softly shaped lips parted beneath the firm pressure of his. Breathtaking pleasure rushed over
and through her as if liquid fire flowed through her veins. . .

D0034306

A CANDLELIGHT ECSTASY ROMANCE ®

NO PROMISE GIVEN

Donna Kimel Vitek

A CANDLELIGHT ECSTASY ROMANCE ®

Published by
Dell Publishing Co., Inc.
1 Dag Hammarskjold Plaza
New York, New York 10017

ISBN: 0–440–16077–4

Printed in the United States of America
First printing—August 1983

For my cousin Lynette Smith Steck.
With thanks to Jean Stanton.

To Our Readers:

We have been delighted with your enthusiastic response to Candlelight Ecstasy Romances®, and we thank you for the interest you have shown in this exciting series.

In the upcoming months we will continue to present the distinctive sensuous love stories you have come to expect only from Ecstasy. We look forward to bringing you many more books from your favorite authors and also the very finest work from new authors of contemporary romantic fiction.

As always, we are striving to present the unique, absorbing love stories that you enjoy most—books that are more than ordinary romance.

Your suggestions and comments are always welcome. Please write to us at the address below.

Sincerely,

The Editors
Candlelight Romances
1 Dag Hammarskjold Plaza
New York, New York 10017

CHAPTER ONE

Abby Windsor, smiling, handed a slim file folder to her assistant, Pam. "Run this data through the computer right away, please. I want to take the demographic breakdowns with me when I leave this evening," she said, pretending not to notice the impatient muttering of her friend Faye Howard, who had dropped by the office for a brief visit. As Pam left with the folder, closing the door quietly behind her, Abby settled back in the swivel chair behind her desk, wrinkled her nose almost mischievously at Faye, and gave a brief nod of her head. "Okay, go on. Say what you're thinking."

"You *know* what I'm thinking. Abby, this just won't do. I nearly had to talk myself blue in the face to get you to agree to spend two weeks with David and me at Fairfields. And now look at this," Faye said, dramatically waving one hand over the folders half in and half out of Abby's soft leather briefcase. "You're actually going to take all this with you. I bet you'll work through this whole vacation."

"That's a bet you'll lose, then, because I do plan to relax during the next two weeks," Abby stated emphatically, then chuckled at the extremely doubtful expression that appeared on her friend's face. Amusement danced in her aqua eyes as she touched her fingertips to her sun-streaked honey-blond hair, which was caught neatly in a clasp at her nape. Still smiling, she reinforced her statement with a nod. "Really, Faye, I'm going to have fun during my stay at Fairfields. *But*"—she too swept a hand above the folders in and around the briefcase—"I can't spend every minute of the next fourteen days down lounging on the beach or wandering over Fairfields's grounds. I may even get tired of catching up on my reading, and if I do, I can spend an hour or two once in a while working."

The downcurved corners of Faye's mouth accompanied her slight frown. "It's more likely you'll spend an hour or two now and then relaxing and the rest of the time with your nose buried in those folders."

"It won't be that way."

"You promise?"

"I give you my solemn oath. What more can I say to convince you? Should I swear on a stack of Bibles that I won't spend my vacation working?"

Faye couldn't prevent herself from returning Abby's teasing smile. "No, swearing on a stack of Bibles won't be necessary, I guess. But I have to admit I'd be happier if you'd leave that briefcase and everything in it here in your office while you're staying with us."

"Sorry, but I can't do that," Abby replied, a note of finality in her soft voice that indicated clearly that this particular discussion had ended. Leaning forward over her desk again, she automatically made a neat stack of the folders to slip them in to the leather case. Then, with an unapologetic shrug, she looked steadily at Faye. "Only three weeks after my vacation, I have to be prepared to present an entire ad campaign down to the smallest detail. Most of the work is done already, but my presentation still needs finishing touches. That's why I have to take all this information with me to Fairfields. I have to start tying up loose ends so this campaign will be letter-perfect. After all, this is the largest and most important account I've ever been allowed to handle, and I can't miss this opportunity to impress my bosses."

"It seems to me you've impressed them plenty already. This is the largest advertising agency in Charleston, and you've been an account executive for a year now, though you're only twenty-six. Obviously, your bosses are very pleased with you."

"So far. But you're mistaken. I was only promoted to account executive about six months ago, and I assure you my superiors are still keeping a close eye on me," Abby corrected absently as she searched her top desk drawer for a survey she absolutely had to take with her to Fairfields. "And until they have complete faith in my abilities, I can't afford to get careless with any account they assign me. In other words, I have to try to do a perfect job every time."

"And no doubt you succeed," Faye commented while examining her neatly manicured nails. "I can't imagine you performing any task carelessly. To tell the truth, sometimes I wonder if you're one of those true perfectionists."

Abby laughed. "Oh, I don't think I am. I just like to be as precise as possible."

"You know, some people almost seem driven to do everything perfectly, as if they're trying to run away from something they don't want to face. Maybe they keep themselves so busy with even the most minor details that they are able to avoid confronting something they can't bear to think about," Faye said, her conversational tone altering as she added, "You don't feel driven that way, do you, Abby?"

"And what kind of question is that?" Abby asked, managing to sustain her smile, although, when she looked up she found Faye regarding her with rather piercing speculation. She tensed slightly but pretended not to notice her friend's sudden air of solemnity. "Of course I don't feel driven. I don't think I *have* to do everything perfectly. I just like to do the best I can as often as possible. Nothing wrong in that, is there?"

"No. But—"

"I'm beginning to suspect you're trying some amateur psychoanalysis on me," Abby interrupted with a forced grin. "Fascinating as this conversation is, though, I'm afraid we'll have to postpone finishing it. If you want me to get to Fairfields by eight for dinner tonight, I have to chase you out of here now so I can get back to work."

"Well, I know a hint when I hear one," Faye joked, a more characteristic smile reappearing to grace her face again. She stood and strolled to the office door but stopped to look back while brushing a hand over her cap of auburn hair, which feathered prettily across her forehead. Her eyes didn't directly meet Abby's when she added, seemingly as an afterthought, "Oh, by the way, have you seen Joel lately?"

The mere mention of that name caused a swift and painful constriction in Abby's throat. Her heartbeat altered to heavy, desolate thudding, yet there was not one iota of discernible change in her composed expression as she shook her head. "No, I have not seen Joel and I don't expect to be seeing him. I told you it was all over between us."

"I know what you told me, but I still think it's a pity," Faye persisted, watching intently as Abby also stood and came around her desk. "You and Joel were so perfect together, like you were made for each other. Everybody thought so."

"Then obviously everybody was wrong," Abby replied with a glibness she certainly didn't feel. "If we had been that perfect together, we wouldn't have gone our separate ways, would we?" Giving Faye no chance to answer that rhetorical question, she advanced toward the door. "Now I really have to get busy or I'll be working so late tonight that I won't make it out to Fairfields until tomorrow."

"All right, all right, I'm going," Faye said good-naturedly, turning. "See you for dinner, then."

"Yes, dinner," Abby repeated cheerily, but as the door closed behind the older woman her smile faded to nonexistence, and it was as if a sudden shadow darkened her eyes to pools of deep blue. She sighed, unconsciously flicking an imaginary piece of lint from her tailored suit, which covered, but couldn't conceal, the eye-catching feminine curvature of her slender body. For several long seconds she stood immobile, staring at the floor, then she abruptly curled her hands into tight fists and softly swore. She could not think about Joel anymore. With grim resolve she thrust memories of him far to the back of her mind where she usually kept them confined . . . except when sleeping. And it was bad enough to dream about him almost every night. She couldn't allow herself to think about him now, simply because Faye had mentioned his name.

Abby smiled fondly, concentrating on her friend instead. She had met Faye when they were fellow volunteers in the pediatrics ward of the medical center, and at first it appeared they had little in common. Faye was older by four years and a wife and mother; Abby had always been single, in a sense married to her career. Yet the two of them had become close friends. But now, as she stood in her office, Abby wondered if maybe she had revealed too much of herself to Faye in the six months they had known each other. Or perhaps Faye possessed simply a rare sense of perception. Perhaps she had *known* how precisely on target she had been when she had asked Abby if she felt driven, insinuating that she sought perfection in everything she attempted as an escape from a problem she couldn't bear to deal with. In actuality, it wasn't quite that simple. Nothing ever is. Yet Abby *did* feel driven. Intrinsically honest, she could admit that, but only to herself. No one else must know that because she was trying to compensate for an unpleasant reality over which she had no control, she felt compelled to strive for perfection in every controllable aspect of her life.

The compulsion had begun as a certain gnawing sense of inadequacy that had been quickly overpowered by a pointless anger at the unfairness of it all. She had felt so cheated from the moment she had learned the irrevocable truth about herself: that she had indeed inherited from her mother the defective gene medical science was powerless to correct. That knowledge had constantly tormented her at first, but gradually, as time passed and healed her wounds until only scars were left, she had begun to accept what could not be changed. More important, she had accepted herself as she was. But meeting Joel had changed everything. During her relationship with him, and since it had ended four months ago, acceptance of her fate had become nearly impossible. The old wounds had been re-opened, and this time the healing process was proving to be excruciatingly slow.

The anger and hurt were beginning to fade again, though. Mentally repeating that now in an attempt at self-reassurance, Abby willed away the tears that threatened before they even had a chance to form in her eyes. With a resolute squaring of her shoulders, she opened her door to smile at Pam, who immediately looked up from her desk in the outer office.

"Better come in here. We have a lot to go over this afternoon," Abby said, forcing enthusiasm until it became genuine. And when she and her assistant began discussing matters Pam would have to attend to alone during the next two weeks, Abby started to feel safely in control of her life again. Throughout the past few months it had been mainly thoughts about Joel that had made her feel helpless. Yet she knew how to avoid that feeling: if she occupied her mind fully with other matters, she would have no time to think of him. That was the way she wanted it, the way it had to be. Otherwise, she wouldn't be able to enjoy even a moment's peace.

Leaving Charleston proper and its heavy flow of traffic behind, Abby leisurely drove her red Omni along Highway 17 toward the turnoff that would lead her to Fairfields. It was after seven already. She had stayed at the office later than she had planned to, rushed home to finish packing, and was only now beginning to relax from the hectic pace of the day. Fresh air rushed in her open window, lifting her unconfined hair and swirling random strands against her cheeks. Futilely brushing them back into place, she inhaled the breeze she imagined already possessed a hint of salty scent. Detained by a red light, a sudden thought made Abby snap her fingers and reach into the briefcase on the seat beside her. Searching for the demographic breakdown she was afraid she might have inadvertantly left in her office, she winced and swiftly jerked her hand out from inside the case. A paper cut had produced a tiny slit in the tip of one finger, and as a droplet of blood rose to the surface of her skin, she shuddered. Although she was not at all an overly squeamish person, sometimes even an insignificant incident like this brought back jarring memories. Too often she had seen such a minor cut or even the slightest bruise cause her uncle Ted, her mother's younger brother, to be rushed away in a screeching ambulance to the hospital for countless transfusions. Those traumatic scenes had etched themselves into her memory and were even now occasionally replayed in frightening nightmares.

Yet, Abby wouldn't allow herself to dwell on the tragedy of it. After all, she was fortunate in one aspect: she possessed only the defective gene that caused the affliction;

17

she was female and therefore was not cursed with the affliction herself. After wrapping a tissue around her finger, which caused the bleeding to immediately cease, she waited for the light to switch to green while concentrating determinedly on how to best spend every moment of her well-earned vacation.

The sun was lower in the sky when Abby turned off 17 onto Bohicket Road and soon crossed over the bridge spanning the Atlantic Intracoastal Waterway. The predominantly straight road stretching out ahead and the overhanging branches, festooned with lacy Spanish moss, were soothing to the spirit, and Abby began to hum. Beyond the line of trees bordering the highway the flat countryside still basked unshadowed in the setting sun's amber glow. Minimarshes sporadically dotted the dark loamy earth, and where the land had been left undisturbed, tall trees decorated with tendrils of moss towered above tangled undergrowth. Now a distinct salty scent was accompanying the gentle breeze, and anticipation mounted in Abby as she veered off the road onto a narrow lane about a hundred yards before the sign that pointed the way to Kiawah Island, a private resort.

A double-file vanguard of sprawling ancient live oaks greeted her, standing sentinel along both sides of the lane, their thick overhanging limbs meeting and entangling in a filigree canopy of green. After following the private avenue for over a quarter of a mile, Abby rounded a gentle curve, smiling as Faye and David's lovely restored mansion rose majestically before her. Once one of the largest rice plantations in the South, Fairfields had miraculously escaped total destruction during the Civil War only to begin to fall into ruin in the impoverished years following the conflict. Eventually the main house had been deserted and, when Faye had happened upon it six years ago, it had looked lost and forlorn amidst a tangle of encroaching weeds. The basic structure remained sound, however, and

18

after convincing David to buy it, Faye had set about restoring it to its former splendor. Now it was her pride and joy and she had every right to be proud. With monumental effort, she had brought the old place to beautiful life again, and a visit to Fairfields was like taking a step back in time.

Stopping her Omni on the curved pebble driveway, Abby sighed at the loveliness of it. The mellow brick walls of the house contrasted handsomely with the wide white-pillared veranda and, now, in the shadowing twilight, the long, wide expanse of the front lawn extended like a lush carpet of dark green. Formal gardens flanked each side of the house, then continued in back, and Abby detected the mingling fragrances of magnolia and rosemary, oleander and lilac. A sense of peace stole over her as she got out of the car, smiling lazily at the katydids beginning to orchestrate their strange music while she strolled leisurely with her luggage up the wide steps and across the veranda.

Faye herself ushered Abby into the wide front hall. With all the graciousness of a mistress of the manor, she bestowed the perfunctory yet sincere kiss on Abby's cheek, a southern custom that Abby just as sincerely returned.

"Oh, it's great to be here again. Already I feel more relaxed. Every time I drive up and just see this house, it's as if all the tension drains out of me," Abby said, smiling as Faye indicated with a gesture that she should set her luggage next to an antique mahogany-and-tapestry settee. With a lift of her shoulders, Abby breathed a long contented sigh. "I'm so glad now that you convinced me I needed a vacation and that I should spend it here."

Faye gave her guest an exaggerated smug smile, as if silently saying "I told you so," then she directed Abby into the sitting room, where light refracted through the prisms of a crystal chandelier danced on the gleaming hardwood floor. Furnished with authentic period pieces, many of them dating back to pre–Civil War, the sitting room was

19

a perfect representation of a time long past, when life was more leisurely and full of grace. Abby loved this room, in fact, loved the entire house, and she realized how relieved she was to escape for a least a little while the hectic workaday pace of her life in Charleston. An odd happiness filled her, and she smiled again, then took notice of the long, flowing hostess gown Faye was wearing. Abby glanced at her wristwatch. Ten minutes to eight.

"My, it's later than I thought. I'd better take my bags up to my room and dress for dinner."

"Oh, just take off your suit jacket and you'll be fine," Faye insisted. "You know we're really very informal here and, besides, there'll only be the four of us for dinner. Even the kids are visiting David's parents for the next ten days. I told you that. Remember?"

"Umm" was Abby's absent response as she concentrated on the fragile beauty of the scarlet gladioli blooms rising up from a white porcelain vase. Though she heard footsteps advancing toward the sitting room from the main hall, she was too entranced by the lovely blossoms to look up until Faye commented that David had arrived home. With a smile for her friend's husband, Abby immediately turned around. Her breath caught in her chest and her lips seemed frozen in their upcurved position. Her heart was beating with such astounding rapidity that her pulse began pounding loudly, frantically, in her ears. No longer relaxed, Abby felt as if her entire body had become a tight coil as alternating waves of blazing heat and icy cold washed over her. She could hardly believe that this wasn't another of those distressing dreams she frequently endured, because as David entered the room, Abby saw that he was not alone. Joel was with him!

Seeing him so unexpectedly after four months was a blow to Abby, to say the very least. Standing still as a sculpted statue, she could only stare at him, taking in the subtle muscular lineation of his lean body, clad in gray

20

trousers, navy blazer, and a light blue shirt, open at the collar, that accentuated the mahogany tan of his smooth skin. A burning ache radiated through Abby's chest. God! He was the last person in the world she needed to see.

Joel, appropriately enough, seemed as surprised to see Abby. And he appeared less than pleased by this encounter, his brown eyes narrowing, raking over Abby, the muscles in his finely carved jaw tightening perceptibly. Abby felt something akin to nausea stir within her. She could scarcely bear the disdainful expression in his eyes as he looked at her. If only he could know that what she had done had been in *his* best interests. . . .

While the men crossed the room Abby turned an accusing gaze on Faye. "How could you do this?" she whispered so only her friend could hear. "How could you invite him to dinner tonight, while I'm here?"

"David invited him," Faye replied innocently. "Besides, it really isn't such a big deal, is it?"

"I think I should leave right now," Abby muttered through tightly compressed lips.

"Run away, and you'll seem like a coward," Faye warned her pithily, a challenging undertone to her low voice. "You wouldn't want Joel to think you're uncomfortable around him, would you?"

Abby's own strong sense of pride made Faye's argument an effective trap, and she groaned inwardly for walking right into it. Faye was right. She would not, *could* not, leave abruptly simply because Joel was there. That would be an obvious show of weakness, and she must never, ever appear weak to him. With that in mind, she was able to appear outwardly composed as David greeted her fondly while Faye and Joel spoke. Then after David briefly hugged his wife and gave her a kiss, a heavy silence fell over the room.

For an interminable moment Abby and Joel simply looked at each other. Although Abby knew that they

21

couldn't remain immobile much longer, it was actually Joel who made the first move. He stepped toward her, unsmiling, his eyes still hard upon her, but he extended both his hands. "Abby, how are you?"

"Fine. And you?" she responded softly, automatically laying her smaller hands in his, trying not to think of how good it was to touch him again after so many long weeks. Almost as if to prove to herself that she was unafraid of his very physical effect on her, she moved closer, stretched up on tiptoe, and started to lightly kiss his cheek. Her heart skipped several beats when he deliberately turned his head at that same instant and touched his lips to hers instead. A sensation as jolting as an electric shock rushed through her, awakening every nerve ending as she felt that familiar sexual attraction flare between them as hotly as it ever had. Yet, she felt something else, too. Although his lips only met her own lightly, and one large brown hand had come up to only cup her chin lightly, she knew he had never kissed her with less gentleness. The set of his chiseled lips had alerted her to the anger in him.

When Joel released her and turned again to Faye and David, Abby knew his anger was very real and she couldn't really blame him for what he felt. Undoubtedly, Joel Richmond was unaccustomed to young women terminating relationships with him, especially without a word of explanation. Abby had no doubt hurt his pride in a way no woman ever had, because most women found him irresistible. That was understandable. Already a universally respected pediatric surgeon at age thirty-five, he possessed a brilliance that literally shone in his intelligent brown eyes. That brilliance, combined with a natural aura of virility, was enough to make most females feel somewhat weak-kneed. Abby certainly hadn't been immune to his brand of masculinity. And even now, watching him speak to David, she experienced a desire to run her fingers

22

through his dark brown hair. She caught her lower lip between her teeth.

Seeing him again hurt deeply. Faye was right. They had seemed so right for each other. He had introduced himself to her at the hospital where she did volunteer work on weekends, and before their first evening together ended, they both knew their attraction to each other was virtually irrepressible. He was so much fun and such a stimulating conversationalist that it took very little time for her to fall hopelessly in love with him. Even then she fought an intimate involvement, but it was ultimately a battle she couldn't win. Tempted in the past to sleep with other men, Abby had always resisted because the fear of pregnancy was so deeply ingrained in her. With Joel, it had been far different. Her need to give herself completely to him had overcome even the old fear. Their first time together had been a joyous pleasure beyond her wildest dreams. Joel had been surprised but, she knew, secretly pleased by her obvious total lack of experience.

"Why me, Abby?" he had asked, holding her close to him after their lovemaking. "I know other men must have wanted you, but you obviously said no to them. Why did you say yes to me?"

"I guess because you're just too damn sexy, Doctor," she had whispered, avoiding her best opportunity to tell him the truth about herself yet forgetting even to feel guilty as he had kissed her again. And again.

After that night, she had faithfully taken precautions, knowing that their new intimacy would continue. As their relationship deepened she had begun nearly to believe they could actually have a future together. When Joel had asked her to move in with him, she had decided to say she would . . . until that evening when she had met him in his office after the last of his day's appointments. When she had arrived, she had found him in his outer office, cradling a patient no older than six weeks in his arms while the baby's parents beamed gratefully at him. As soon as Abby came to Joel's side he promptly handed her the infant. Gazing down at the chubby face, feeling the baby's soft warm body snuggled against her breasts, Abby had been swamped by a horrid self-pity she had vowed never to indulge in. As soon as possible, without seeming rude, she had transferred the child to the mother's eagerly awaiting arms. Before leaving the office the parents had expressed their sincerest thanks to Joel for successfully performing the difficult surgery that had saved their tiny son's life.

Finally alone with Abby, Joel had turned her to him. "You look very lovely with a baby in your arms," he had said softly, kissing her eyebrows, the hollows of her cheeks, and at last her lips. "Someday, maybe it could be our child you hold. You know, of course, that my father's a surgeon and my brother's a resident in pediatric surgery now. I like to think that my sons might want to carry on the tradition. My daughters too, for that matter."

With his words, Abby's hopes had died. Realizing that Joel specialized in pediatric surgery because he truly loved children, she had known she couldn't move in with him. She had foolishly hoped that their relationship could lead to a childless marriage, but obviously, to him marriage would eventually involve raising a family. And it was a family she couldn't give him. In that moment she had wanted to blurt out the truth but fear of his reaction prevented her. How could she tell him that if she bore him a son, the child would stand a fifty-fifty chance of enduring an average of eight severe bleeding episodes a year—bleeding brought on by nothing more serious than a paper cut on the finger or a light bruise? How could she tell him that if she bore him a daughter, that child would stand a fifty-fifty chance of possessing the defective gene that would pass on the affliction? Those were gambles Abby had long feared she could never take. Joel wouldn't want to take them either. As a pediatric surgeon, he would be well

24

aware of *all* the frightening realities that accompanied hemophilia. Abby hadn't been able to bear the thought of telling him the truth. She had been terrified of the horror she might see in his eyes when she said the word *hemophilia,* and more terrifying had been the possibility that the horror would become pity. And if he knew the truth, he would eventually leave her, because he wanted an involvement with a woman who could give him healthy children. Abby knew how devastating the rejection would be when she ultimately lost Joel after telling him her secret.

During the two weeks following the night in Joel's office Abby had made excuse after excuse not to see him. She had stopped taking his calls at her office, then didn't return them later, feeling that although it was a cowardly way to end their relationship, it was best for both of them. Joel, however, had been persistent. He had arrived uninvited at her apartment late one night, demanding an explanation, and when she had been able to neither tell him the truth nor produce a convincing lie to explain the way she had been acting, his patience had ended. He had left her alone, and Abby hadn't seen him since then.

Until today . . .

Forcibly dragging herself from her reverie, Abby stared with unwitting longing at the broad expanse of Joel's shoulders. His back was to her. He was making no effort to include her in his conversation with Faye and David, and for that, Abby was grateful. She wasn't ready to make idle chitchat. Seeing him here at Fairfields was such a shock that she needed time to try to gather all her inner strength around her like a protective mantle, merely in order to deal with his presence.

Unfortunately, Faye had other ideas. Making a lame excuse about a malfunctioning oven, she practically propelled David out into the hall and rushed him toward the kitchen, leaving Abby and Joel alone in the sitting room.

25

Determined to appear nonchalant, Abby gave Joel an easy smile when he immediately turned toward her. Flicking her hair back over her shoulders, she settled herself comfortably on a damask sofa, surprised by her own acting ability as she strove to seem perfectly relaxed. Unwilling to be the first to terminate the disruptive eye contact with Joel, she continued to look at him while lazily stroking her fingertips over a plush velvet throw pillow. "I really love this house, don't you?" she finally asked, breaking a silence that to her, at least, was becoming almost unbearably tense. "I love visiting here. And it was very considerate of Faye to invite us both for dinner on the same evening so that neither of us has to feel like a fifth wheel."

"Faye's a very gracious lady but, actually, I'm not just here for dinner," Joel said, his gaze drifting slowly over Abby. "When I mentioned to David that I planned to take a couple weeks of vacation, he and Faye insisted I spend them here."

Suspicion that was near certainty sparked in Abby's eyes, yet she was able to maintain her relaxed pose on the sofa and inquire, "You're saying you'll be at Fairfields for the next two weeks?" When Joel nodded, she felt as if her stomach had tied itself into a tight knot, but her only outward reaction to his answer was a polite smile. "I'll be here for the next two weeks, too. In fact, Faye begged me to plan my vacation for this particular time."

Joel raised dark eyebrows, and the slight movement of his lips expressed sardonic amusement. "Our Faye's an incurable romantic, it seems. Obviously, she hoped we might resume our relationship if she threw us together for a while. Of course, I'll be a gentleman and leave if it bothers you that I'm here."

If it bothered her . . . Abby felt a sudden crazy inclination to laugh and cry at the same time. This situation was insane. Of course Joel *bothered* her. For weeks she had been trying not to think about him, and now he was here in the flesh, occupying her every thought. She could imagine how spending two entire weeks under the same roof with him would tear her emotions to shreds all over again, but he was treating her with such cold disdain right now that she was overwhelmed by a driving need to prove she could be as cold as he was. She tossed one hand in a careless gesture of dismissal and laughed shortly. "Why, Joel, what a crazy notion," she drawled, stretching her acting ability to the limit. "Why should it bother me if you're here? After all, I'd really like to consider us still friends."

"We were a hell of a lot more than friends. We were lovers, Abby" was his quick retort as, without warning, he sat down onto the sofa beside her, his powerful body dangerously tensed. Imprisoning her in the corner by reaching across her to grip the right armrest and placing his other hand just above her left shoulder, he leaned nearer her. "And neither friends nor lovers end a relationship without reason. Tell me what yours was."

He was too close. Inwardly Abby trembled. She could detect the too deliciously familiar scent of his spicy aftershave and see the faint traces of a day's growth of beard on his jaw. She ached to touch him yet was terrified he might touch her. Her throat was suddenly dry and it was difficult to swallow, but she willed her shoulders to rise and fall in a tiny shrug. "I really didn't plan on ending anything," she lied. "I was just so involved with my work; there was so much to do that I never seemed to have any spare time to—"

"You weren't working any harder or longer at the end of our relationship than at the beginning, so why don't you finally tell me the truth," Joel commanded after causing her words to trail off midsentence when she saw the fiery glint of light that abruptly appeared in his eyes. Smiling rather unpleasantly at the ease with which he'd silenced

27

her, he leaned closer. His warm breath fanned her cheek as he dropped his hand down onto her shoulder and brushed the edge of his thumb over the delicate curve of her neck. "You didn't stop seeing me because you were working too hard. Maybe you just got bored. Maybe you didn't find the satisfaction you needed. Was that it? Didn't I measure up as a lover?"

"How the hell would I know?" Abby shot back, enraged that during the past months while she had been going through agony because she had lost him, he had been merely nursing a bruised ego. Bitterness and hurt rose in her, gathering in a lump in her throat as her own eyes flashed blue fire at him. "Maybe you're a satisfactory lover, maybe not. I couldn't say, since there never was any other man to compare you with. And you know that, Joel."

"I only know I was your first lover," he muttered, fingertips pressing down into the flesh of her shoulder to the delicate bone structure. "How can I be sure you didn't become involved with someone else while you were still seeing me?"

"You can't be sure," Abby retorted sharply, suppressing the desire to flail her fists at him for even insinuating she had betrayed him, as much as she had loved him! Flexing her shoulder in an effort to escape his hard grip, she sighed impatiently when he refused to release her. "Is there another reason for this dramatic little episode, or are you really only asking my evaluation of you as a bedmate?"

"Something like that. Call it curiosity if you like," Joel said with unabashed candor, his gaze devoid of emotion as it captured and held hers. "I'm a man who tries to learn from experience, and if our lovemaking didn't satisfy you, I'd like you to tell me what mistakes I made. That way I can avoid making the same ones with other women."

If he was deliberately trying to wound and humiliate, he

was making a tremendous success of it. At the thought of him with other women, Abby felt physically ill. His hands on her became a torment, evoking mental images of those same hands caressing other bodies—bodies of any number of women who could give him everything she had ever given him, plus the children he wanted but that she could never bear. A very basic jealousy of those unknown women ripped through her chest, and the little charade she had been so valiantly acting out began to quickly crumble around the edges. She knew she could endure little more of this emotional torture and prepared to surrender in their verbal battle while she still had a chance to emerge with most of her pride and dignity intact.

"I think you know very well that you are expert enough in lovemaking to satisfy any woman," she answered at last, averting her gaze, although she miraculously kept her voice steady and clear. "If you made any mistakes, I don't remember them."

"I satisfied you, then?" he persisted in a deep, husky, dizzyingly seductive whisper. "After you ended everything, I began to wonder if maybe your passionate response to me had really always been pretense." One lean finger lifted Abby's chin, forcing her to face him directly again. He regarded her intently. "Even now I wonder, and there's only one way to know for certain."

"No!" Abby gasped. Warned too late by that swift blazing of passion in his piercing eyes that she had seen so often and known so well, she scarcely had a chance to throw her hands defensively against his broad chest before his muscular arms were around her, crushing her to him. With little effort, he drew her hands down and around his waist while impelling her backward into the softness of the sofa cushion. He had proven his physical superiority in an instant, yet she could still have resisted him emotionally had he been brutal. Except for the conquering roughness of the initial embrace, however, he seduced her with tenderness, ignoring her puny attempts at resistance as he lightly kissed her eyelids, the contours of her high cheekbones, and the sensitized scented hollows beneath her ears. Joel's long strong fingers glided through the silken strands of her hair, tangling them as he cradled the back of her head in his palm. The moment he felt the tension melting from her, he molded her gracefully curved body to the hard length of his, then began to mercilessly tease first one corner of her mouth, then the other with featherlight kisses.

Unshed tears were pinpricks behind Abby's eyes as she helplessly drifted down, down into the dreamy lethargy he could always induce in her. It was so good to be held by him again. She had missed his warmth for so many long nights and had ached for the searing heat of his desire, which had always aroused her own to intolerable heights. Now she knew she was a fool to succumb to his caresses and kisses but was unable to force herself to push away from him. And as he continued to tease the corners of her mouth she made a soft sound that was almost a whimper. She heard his low triumphant laugh, but all that mattered at that moment was that he really kiss her, and when he did, she kissed him back with an ardor that erupted from the innermost core of her being. Her softly shaped lips parted beneath the firm pressure of his, and when his teeth closed gently on the lower curve, her mouth opened. The tip of her tongue met his. Breathtaking pleasure rushed over and through her, kindling wildfires on every inch of her skin, and it was as if liquid fire flowed in her veins.

Abby's arms wrapped tightly around Joel's waist, her hands, on his back, pressing him harder against her. He touched her full, tautly strained breasts as he kissed her again and again, and when his hand beneath her hips arched her lower body up against his muscular thighs and his potent masculinity, she involuntarily moved nearer.

"You weren't pretending then. You aren't pretending

now," he whispered hoarsely, his warm breath caressing her inner ear. "You've missed this, Abby."

"No," she denied vehemently.

"Little liar," he taunted, his own words muffled as he kissed her once again with rousing, marauding insistence. A lean hand slipped between her shapely thighs beneath her skirt and began an agonizingly slow upward glide. "You want me as much as I want you."

The more intimate caress brought Abby to her senses. She caught his wrist, stilling his hand before putting it away from her completely. She shifted herself, creating some distance between them. "Stop. Now," she demanded, though with some shortness of breath. "This is crazy. Faye and David could walk back in here at any minute."

"It isn't exactly the proper time or place, is it?" he commented offhandedly, regarding her with a sensuous smile. "But I'm sure we can arrange it so that we're alone together often during the next two weeks."

Heaving an inward sigh, Abby smoothed her tousled hair and shook her head. "I don't think so, Joel."

His eyebrows lifted. "No? Ah, but it will be such a waste if we don't spend as much time as possible alone, considering how much fun we always had together. It's obvious you aren't interested in a serious relationship, and frankly, I'm not either, so with no strings attached, no commitments, we can just relax and thoroughly enjoy each other during this vacation."

"Sort of make it a sex holiday?" Abby asked woodenly, warmth rising in her cheeks when his muted, deep-throated, and almost mocking laughter was directed at her. She lifted her small chin defensively. "Is that what you're suggesting?"

"Well, I wouldn't be so blunt as to call it a sex holiday. But think how much more we both can enjoy our vacations if we spend a good part of the time making love."

Her eyes quickly scanned his lean sun-browned face,

searching for some show of affection in his expression. She found none. He was merely surveying her with an obvious appreciation of feminine sexuality. Her heart suddenly felt heavy, like a stone in her breast. Apparently she had overestimated the depth of his feelings for her and, somehow, that depressed her terribly, though it really shouldn't have. After all, she had been the one to end their relationship. She should be relieved he had suffered no more than a minor blow to his masculine pride. Yet, she wasn't relieved. She felt incongruously betrayed . . . because in this scant half hour she had been forced to accept the fact that her feelings for him were as strong as ever. That gave him an advantage, and she knew it. With a look, a touch, a kiss, he might be able to seduce her some time during the next two weeks. And he was certainly giving her every indication that seduction was what he had in mind.

Abby stared silently at him, her emotions too overwrought for her to speak. She was so caught up in involuntarily studying the clean-cut features of his beloved face that she wasn't even aware of Faye's and David's return to the room until Joel smiled enigmatically at her, then rose to his feet. When Joel strode to the freestanding bar to join David, acting for all the world as if nothing had happened between Abby and him during their hosts' absence, she allowed herself to release a long shuddering breath. She barely noticed Faye's questioning stare and didn't respond to it. She simply sat immobile on the sofa, hands clenched tightly in her lap.

Conflicting emotions pulled her in all directions. Part of her wanted to speed hastily back to Charleston, to escape Joel by retreating, however cowardly that might appear. But her stupid pride would never allow her to do that. The knowledge that Joel's interest in her had never been much more than sexual evoked an intense need to spend the next two weeks pretending he meant no more to her than she did to him—no easy task. Could her already tattered emotions withstand the monumental effort she would have to put in to presenting a convincing performance?

That was a question to which Abby had no answer. At that moment she was so filled with confusion, everything in her life seemed turned upside down. All she knew for certain was that Faye had a strange conception of what would be a relaxing vacation for Abby. With Joel at Fairfields too, Abby knew she couldn't reasonably expect to experience many moments, if any, of real peace and tranquillity.

CHAPTER TWO

The next morning, Abby padded across the damp sand onto the drier stretch of beach where she had earlier spread a large towel. Her rate of breathing was just now beginning to decelerate as she wrapped the thick swath of her hair around one hand to squeeze out as much water as possible. She sank down on to her knees on the sun-warmed terry fabric, then stretched out on her stomach, extending her arms straight down and close against her body. Her heart still beat hard and fast, but she had spent nearly forty-five minutes battling the rushing waves, swimming out again and again against the oncoming water, then allowing the swells to carry her back into the frothy swirls of the foaming surf licking the shore. Abby had always enjoyed swimming, but that morning the exercise had been more therapeutic than recreational. Nervous tension had built up in her to almost an explosive level, but now, for the first time since seeing Joel the previous night, she actually felt relaxed. Physical exertion can serve as a very effective emotional safety valve, Abby thought as she smiled with relief, noting that even the nervous fluttering of her stomach had ceased.

Closing her eyes against the dazzling glare of the bleached white beach, she nuzzled her cheek against the towel, creating a small comfortable hollow in the sand beneath. Lulled by the hypnotic regularity of the lapping surf as it tumbled in, then receded, she banished all thoughts from her mind. Having spent a torturously restless night, she soon drifted into that comforting gray zone midway between wakefulness and sleep, where the gentle breaking of the waves and the faint calls of distant sandpipers contributed to a much-needed sense of security and peace.

Some time later, having no idea how long she had floated in that semiaware state, Abby came slowly to the realization that the sun was no longer burning with bright intensity against her closed eyelids. Its warming rays no longer toasted her back either. She was lying in a shadow and, wondering if a potentially dangerous storm cloud was passing over, she reluctantly forced her thickly lashed eyelids to flutter open. Aqua eyes widened momentarily before drifting upward, following the masculine contours of long muscular legs covered with fine dark hair, up past lean hips clad in navy swimming trunks and the broad expanse of a bronze chest. It was a body she knew well, and before her eyes traveled farther upward to meet his narrowed brown ones, she was well aware that it was Joel who towered above her.

For a tense moment that seemed to last an eternity Joel looked down at Abby expressionlessly. Then a somewhat mysterious smile curved his lips, etching faint but incredibly attractive indentations on each side of his mouth, and he lowered himself down in a sitting position beside her on the towel. His gaze roamed over her, frankly admiring shapely lightly tanned long legs and the curvaceous contours outlined against the clinging fabric of a cherry-red maillot swimsuit. If he was aware of how disconcerting his unabashed appraisal was, he didn't seem to care as he closely watched Abby turn over and prop herself up on her elbows next to him.

"Is this where you've been all morning?" he asked, reaching behind Abby to pluck a sea oat from the sand. "At breakfast Faye wondered where you'd disappeared to. She seemed a little worried."

"I should have left a note," Abby admitted, but didn't add she had been in such a rush to escape the house and him that writing Faye a note had never occurred to her. "Faye didn't need to be concerned, though. She knows I have a tendency to wander around when I visit Fairfields. This morning I just woke up with the beach on my mind. And you have to come early to find the nicest seashells."

Joel nodded wordlessly, turning his head to stare out over the ocean before a frown creased his brow and he returned his gaze to Abby. He surveyed her hair, then reached out to lift a still-damp strand. "Your hair's wet. You've been in the water," he said disapprovingly. "Surely you know it's very dangerous to swim alone."

"I just couldn't resist this time," Abby confessed, strongly touched because he had expressed some concern for her well-being. Afraid he might be able to detect a revealing gratitude mirrored in eyes that had always been far too expressive, she looked away from him and stared instead at her own hand as she scooped up sand and allowed it to sift slowly between her fingers. "And I am a pretty good swimmer."

"Good swimmer or not, you never know what kind of unexpected trouble you might get into, so promise you won't go out in the water by yourself again."

"Okay, okay, I promise," she conceded indignantly. "It *is* foolish to swim alone." Her smile masked a slight confusion. Had she only imagined she'd heard a hint of anxiety in his deep voice, or had it really been there? If so, why? The night before, he had acted as if he didn't give a damn about her, as if she were no more to him than a sex object.

36

But thus far that morning she had seen no evidence of such a demeaning attitude toward her. She smiled ruefully to herself. The morning was young yet, and it would hardly be wise to assume that he wouldn't revert to the previous night's harsh behavior. In the hope that he wouldn't, though, she searched her brain for some topic of conversation that would be neither provocative nor boring. As it turned out Joel saved her the trouble of thinking of one.

"How's the job?" he asked her. "Any interesting new clients?"

When she answered in the affirmative but didn't elaborate, he pressed her for details and, as she warmed to the subject, listened to her with sincere interest. The questions he asked about the agency were pertinent and knowledgeable, because he obviously had not forgotten anything he had learned from her about the advertising game. His attentiveness allowed her to thoroughly enjoy discussing her career with him. When she had described almost every important incident that had occurred at the agency in the past four months, she inquired about his practice.

As always when he discussed his profession, his dedication to medicine was unmistakable. Perfectly relaxed now, Abby sat cross-legged on the towel, hands palm down close beside her, unable to tear her gaze from him as he poignantly told her about some of his young patients. Her eyes roved wonderingly over his strong, intelligent face, catching the sometimes sadly resigned expression that fleetingly passed over it, catching the more frequent indications that he found true gratification in what he did. Now he had become again the man she had known four months ago, and she was assailed by powerful emotions she didn't dare define. Joel, as he was that morning, was irresistibly intriguing, but never for a moment could Abby allow herself to forget that nothing had changed. Her genetic legacy hadn't miraculously been altered, and never would be—a fact that was almost easier to accept when

Joel treated her disdainfully as he had the previous night. That morning he was so attractive, so endearing, that emotional and physical longing were rapidly intensifying to agonizing keenness—a feeling she could not allow. When Joel noticed how somberly she was watching him, his piercing dark eyes abruptly impaled hers and he reached out as if to touch her.

"Let's swim," she suggested swiftly, jumping to her feet, waiting expectantly for him to get up, too. He did but looked down at her so soberly that she was certain he was on the verge of saying something she was afraid to hear. She gave him no chance to speak by immediately rushing off across the beach and babbling back over her shoulder, "The water's incredibly warm this morning. You'll love it."

As the waves splashed her smooth thighs Abby glanced back and saw Joel ankle-deep in the surface, tan hands on lean hips as he followed her every movement. His very stance conveyed annoyance, and she looked forward again. She trudged on into deeper water, the edge of her teeth sinking into her lower lip. She realized how erratic her behavior must seem to Joel, but she was powerless to remedy any part of the entire ironic situation. That old feeling of utter helplessness threatened to overwhelm her, but she fought it by diving into the water and coming up for air in a brisk scissor stroke, swimming diagonally against the force of the incoming waves. She went out some distance to where the water was more placid. Flipping onto her back, she floated, closing her eyes against the bright sun. Eventually the waves carried her close to shore, but before she could be tumbled in the breakers, she turned and swam back out to begin the process again. She saw Joel slice through the water beyond her, but if he noticed her, he gave no indication. She turned over onto her back once more. For a long time she was left alone and *felt* lonely. When she neared the shore, she turned back,

38

walking until her feet no longer touched bottom. Bored with floating, she simply trod water while staring at the far horizon.

A few minutes later, when Joel's arms suddenly encircled her waist, Abby was so startled, she stiffened and nearly went under. His hold on her tightened, drawing her fast against him, preventing her from slipping beneath the surface. Her hands automatically gripped his shoulders. His nearness caused her heart to thud so violently that she almost imagined he could hear it over the ocean's roar. Tall enough to touch bottom, Joel easily held her up and smiled rather wickedly.

"You're being lazy, Abby, just floating around out here," he said softly. "Swimming is supposed to be good exercise, but I think you need some incentive to get you moving."

When he promptly started pulling her toward shore, she tried in vain to tell him that she had spent forty-five minutes of nearly nonstop swimming already that morning. He acted as if he didn't hear a word. When the water was no more than waist-high on Joel, he unceremoniously swept Abby up in his arms. Ignoring her protests, he watched until a high, sweeping swell rolled toward them, timed his move, then tossed her directly into it.

The wave caught Abby perfectly, breaking in a cascading frothy rush over her, tumbling her head over heels until she was ignominiously deposited on the beach in the soft foaming surf. Spluttering, she raised herself up on her hands and knees, glowering back at Joel, avenging intent evident in the very set of her chin. To retaliate for the sand now in her hair, she scooped up a wet handful and splashed into the water to where Joel stood grinning.

Abby grinned back, brought her hand from behind her, raised it, and plopped the oozing sand with a resounding smack onto his hair-roughened chest. She had to laugh as grainy rivulets trickled slowly down over his flat abdo-

39

men. "There, how do you like having that muck all over you?" she taunted playfully, then beat a hasty retreat when he began advancing on her, evil intent glinting in his eyes.

Over a half hour later Abby formally conceded defeat. Joel was too strong, too fast for her to possibly beat in a water fight, and when she at last laughingly raised her hands in surrender just as he was about to dunk her again, he proved to be a gracious victor. Going ahead of her as they waded out of the surf, he went for a towel and came back to meet her with it as she slowly followed after him.

Abby smiled her thanks. After blotting her face and shoulders dry, she grimaced. "The ocean is terrific except for the salt the water leaves on your skin. What I really need is a shower. I feel so sticky."

Without a word Joel caught her hand in his and led her beyond the patch of sea oats toward Faye and David's small bungalow, constructed of diagonal weathered gray boards. An outside shower had been rigged above a low wood-slatted platform, and Joel and Abby stepped up on it together. Reaching up, he pulled a chain, smiling at her sharp gasp when a strong spray of unexpectedly cold water peppered both of them.

Despite the shivers that occasionally ran over her, Abby delighted in the rinsing off. Briskly rubbing with her hands, she washed away the salty residue that had clung to her. When every inch of skin on her arms and shoulders and legs felt squeaky clean again, she lifted her face to the spray, rotating her head until her neck and even the area behind her ears felt clean again. She touched her hair, feeling scattered fine grains on her scalp. It would have to wait for a proper shampooing.

As if he were reading her mind, Joel lightly grasped her shoulders and turned her to face him. Lean fingers combed through her hair, gently easing tangles out of the tousled strands, extending each section in its turn until it was

40

directly beneath the spray. Then, catching water in his cupped hands, he sluiced it over her shimmering gold hair until it ran down to fall from individual ends in crystalline droplets.

When Joel began gently massaging Abby's scalp, dislodging the grains of sand, she stood completely still, her head bent, practically mesmerized by the circular strokes of his ministering fingers. She allowed him to move her directly beneath the forceful spray, which rinsed away the last of the sand. Or so she thought. But Joel was a very thorough man. He repositioned her to one side of the shower and brushed the silken swath over across one shoulder as his fingertips searched her nape for any grains that might remain.

"There, that should do it," he said at last, but didn't completely release her.

The moment his hand cupped the back of Abby's neck she trembled violently, as a shattering need to be held in his arms shot like a jolt of electricity through her. Uttering a soft moan, she turned and reached out to him, slender arms wrapping tightly around his neck when he huskily whispered her name and molded her gracefully curved body to the firmer, more muscular lineation of his. Abby sought the rapidly throbbing pulse in his throat and pressed her lips to it. She desperately needed to touch and caress him, and ached for him to touch and caress her. The night before he had been sarcastic, almost cruelly insensitive, and she had been able to resist him. But, now he was the Joel she had fallen in love with, and resistance was impossible. The mere touch of his hand on the back of her neck had caused emotions too long suppressed to overpower all reason. Now she was in his arms again and wanted never to leave them.

Joel brushed aside the straps of Abby's swimsuit, then swept his hands slowly down to span her trim waist, his fingers stroking and massaging as he rained urgent, impas-

41

sioned kisses over her bare shoulders and along the sweep of her slender neck. Her breathing ragged, Abby caught his face between her hands, lifting his head and leaning back slightly to gaze up at him. Fiery desire glowed hotly in the seemingly bottomless depths of his dark eyes while her pupils widened, darkening her own to a glimmering sapphire.

"God, you're beautiful! Kiss me, Abby!" he commanded roughly.

Spellbound, she obeyed. Stretching up on tiptoe, she touched her parted lips to his.

A soft groan rose from deep in Joel's throat and he swiftly gathered her more tightly to him. Hardening lips hungrily captured the full curve of hers, devouring their tenderness with an ever-increasing pressure that was dizzying. Possessive plundering kisses claimed her mouth, released it, then reclaimed it again and again. Melting against him, Abby returned kiss for kiss, responding ardently when the tip of his tongue traced the soft bow shape of her lips, then slipped between them to taste the sweetness of her mouth. Her own tongue invitingly grazed his. Shivers raced up and down her spine. Her fingers tangled in his thick damp hair as exquisite sensations radiated outward from deep within her. When Joel widened his stance, moving her between his taut muscular thighs, she was all yielding, her body pliant in his hands, which feathered over her gently rounded hips and followed the enchanting contours of her shapely waist, stroking upward to linger, his palms curving over the sides of her breasts, which were straining at the pressure of the powerful chest bearing hard against them.

"My sweet Abby," Joel whispered, lowering his dark head to seek with firm lips the shadowed hollow between the delightfully taut mounds of feminine flesh. Another low groan accompanied the sinuous movement of her long smooth legs against his. His hands curved tightly over her

42

hips before he abruptly released her, stepped off the platform, then lifted her down onto the hot sand beside him.

Abby feathered her fingertips along his bare back as his arm around her waist held her close to his side. Following another path that also led to the beach, they walked between swaying stalks of tall pampas grass, their silken plumes rapidly approaching maturation. In a shady spot beyond the beach house David's roan stallion grazed contentedly in a patch of scruffy vegetation.

"Oh, you rode here," Abby said softly. "I should have done that instead of walking down."

Joel's eyes darkened with a certain promise when he looked down at her. "We'll ride back together. But later. Right now I suggest we get out of the sun for a while and go into the bungalow."

Abby halted abruptly, her feet digging into the sand as her heart pounded against her breastbone. Within a split second a myriad of conflicting thoughts flitted through her mind. She recalled the bungalow's casually furnished living room, where matchbook blinds were rolled down to cover the windows, allowing only a bit of sun to filter through. Part of her longed to enter that cool, dark solitude with Joel, but she knew exactly what would happen between them if she did. A caution stronger than her need to be close to him filled her with the haunting memory of the pain she had experienced when she had been forced to end her relationship with Joel. The intimacy they had shared had only intensified that pain one hundredfold, and she didn't think she could bear to begin that process all over again—the intimate involvement, its inevitable end, and the excruciating hurt that followed. Four months ago she had ended everything for Joel's sake and, immediately afterward, had felt she might die of loneliness. By immersing herself in work she had endured it, but even becoming a full-fledged workaholic might not be effective therapy again. If she drifted into a new involvement with him now, she doubted she could bear to face the inescapable way it would end. She might emerge so embittered by a fate that made her deny herself the person most precious in her life that she would never feel a moment's peace ever again. And Abby didn't want to spend her life embittered.

A chill spread within her, its icy tentacles entwining around her heart. A coolness, born of necessity and some desperation, shone frostily in her blue eyes as she looked up at Joel and shook her head. "I'd rather go back down on the beach. It's a glorious day. Silly to spend it cooped up in the bungalow."

"Abby—"

"No, Joel," she interrupted succinctly, a protective cold demeanor concealing all the inner unhappiness she felt. "I'm just not interested in going into the beach house."

"That's certainly not the impression you were giving me a few minutes ago," he snapped. "The way you were kissing me indicated you would probably be very happy to spend a few hours alone with me there."

Abby managed a seemingly unconcerned shrug. "You got the wrong impression, then."

Joel's arm dropped away from her as he uttered an explicit curse. "What the hell's happened to you, Abby? If you've started to get some kick out of being a tease, try your tricks on somebody else next time, because you'll live to regret it if you ever try them again on me." His jaw clenched, Joel raked a harsh gaze over her from head to foot. "We've both had enough of the beach. We'll go back to the main house. I'll give you a ride."

"No, thanks, I'll walk back."

"You'll ride with me," he nearly growled. "It's a long way, and you've been swimming all morning . . . well, most of it. Anyway, I can see you're tired."

Suddenly she did feel weighted down by an excessive weariness and, too emotionally drained to argue further with him, she nodded reluctantly. "But I left my sunglasses and another towel on the beach. First I'll have to get them."

"I'll get them," Joel muttered, and left her without a backward glance.

The moment he was beyond the patch of sea oats Abby rushed away along the marsh-bordered lane she had walked from the main house earlier that morning. She hoped Joel would decide it wasn't worth his effort to come after her, because if he returned to the house by taking the riding trail, she wouldn't have to bear his contemptuous silence during the eternity the ride home along the lane would take.

Unfortunately, Abby's hopes were dashed within minutes. Her heart thudded almost painfully when she heard the thundering of hooves on the road behind her. She stopped, reluctantly turned, and was unable to look directly at Joel when he reined in the stallion beside her. As the horse tossed its sleek head with an impatient whinny, Joel leaned down, swiftly encircled Abby's waist with one muscular arm, and lifted her easily onto the saddle in front of him.

"Damn it, Abby," he swore roughly, hitting his heels against the roan stallion's sides. "What the hell's your problem?"

Abby said nothing, and the horse broke into a smooth gallop. Clutching the pommel tightly with both hands, Abby stared straight ahead. Tears filled her eyes, causing the overhanging cypress leaves dripping with Spanish moss to become blurs of brown overlaying green. Pain welled up in her and, with it, a certain anger. Telling Joel about her very real and unsolvable problem was precisely what she could never do.

It was after eleven o'clock that evening when Faye and David decided to retire for the night. Noticing the yawn David tried unsuccessfully to hide behind one hand, Abby

45

found herself yawning in response and eased forward onto the edge of the sofa she shared with Joel.

"I'm calling it a day, too," she announced, starting to stand. "I think I'll go on up to my room."

"Don't let her do it, Joel!" Faye warned with a fond smile, though her tone was perfectly serious. "She'll go to her room, but she won't go to bed. Instead, she'll stick her head in that briefcase of hers and work half the night. And I invited her here to relax, not to slave over some presentation she doesn't have to make until weeks from now. So keep her down here, Joel, and try to take her mind off that infernal job of hers . . . somehow."

"No. He doesn't have to do that," Abby protested, unwilling to be foisted onto him. Noting Faye's adamant expression, she breathed a resigned sigh and nodded. "All right, all right. I'll go up to my room and either read or go straight to bed. I won't do any work, I promise."

"I don't believe you," Faye said bluntly, as only a close friend can. With lips pursed disapprovingly, she turned her attention to Joel again. "She just got here last night, but already this afternoon she sneaked into her room and had papers strewn out all over her bed. I caught her."

"I didn't sneak," Abby argued, laughing. "I simply went to my room to glance at some data."

"You weren't just glancing. You were about to settle down to work for hours," Faye insisted, even as her husband took her by one elbow to steer her toward the doorway. Slowly but surely directed out of the room, she flung one last look back at Joel. "I don't want her to work all night. She's supposed to be on vacation. And besides, I'll need her help tomorrow with some preparations for the Magnolia Ball. She won't be much good to me if she's dragging from lack of sleep. Take her for a walk in the gardens or something until she's too tired to think of working when she goes to her room."

"Really, Faye, Joel doesn't have to entertain me," Abby

called after her friend, who was now out in the hall. "Maybe there's something else he'd rather do."

"Never argue with your hostess. Especially if your hostess is Faye Howard. You can't win," Joel said softly beside her, rising lithely to his feet. Reaching down, he took Abby's left hand in his right and drew her up to him. "Come on. Let's see the gardens."

Realizing he could be as insistent as Faye and as unlikely to take no for an answer, Abby nodded and went with him out the French doors onto the veranda. After walking down a wide flight of steps at the east end, they stepped onto one of the garden's main pebbled paths. A delightfully cool breeze that whispered in the high boughs of the cypress and live oak trees also drifted down to stir tendrils of Abby's hair. She brushed them back from her cheek and gazed silently up at the black velvet star-sparkled sky. It was a lovely night for a walk in the gardens. The light of a full yellow moon bathed the earth in a golden hue and was reflected here and there on the smooth surfaces of glossy magnolia and holly leaves as they shifted in the breeze. The fragrances of the day's open blossoms still lingered faintly in the air but were nearly overpowered by the headier scent of the night-blooming cereus.

Despite the loveliness of the surroundings, however, Abby couldn't think of anything to say now that she was alone with Joel. After the morning's debacle, she had done everything possible to avoid him that afternoon, and during dinner they had been highly convincing in the charade they played. It had been as if by silent mutual agreement that they chose not to reveal to their host and hostess the tension that lay between them. It had been there, however, just beneath the surface of seemingly companionable conversation and the joking comments they had occasionally managed to exchange. Abby had tried to forget the abysmal way their morning together had ended, but it was to no avail until the meal was over and the two couples had

47

engaged in a lively game of bridge. Usually Abby was no more than an adequate player, but Joel had been her partner. Their thoughts had seemed so synchronized that they had made few mistakes. Amid moans and groans from Faye and David, Joel and Abby had been incredibly attuned to each other's strategies and had won handily. Immersed in the intense yet friendly competition, Abby had felt perfectly relaxed. But now the game had ended; Faye and David had left her alone with Joel, and the tension was like an oppressive cloud gathering around her again. Glancing sideways at him, taking in his tall broad form silhouetted in moonlight, Abby wondered what he was thinking, yet didn't dare ask.

Although Joel kept Abby's hand lightly enclosed in his, he was obviously in no mood to make conversation either. For a full five minutes the silence dragged on between them as they followed the path that meandered through the side gardens, which really continued uninterrupted around to the back of the house, where flowers and shrubs flourished in even more riotous profusion. To the right a roofed passageway formed a cloister, walled on one side, which opened on the other side onto an intriguing colonnade. And it was only when Abby moved eagerly to the cereus vines twining upward on the brick wall, then lifted a blossom to her face to revel in the exotic fragrance, that Joel spoke for the first time since they had left the house. Even then, the low tone of his deep voice rendered his words indistinguishable as he reached above Abby's head to pluck an exquisite moonflower from the vine. Releasing Abby's hand, he proceeded to tuck the bloom into her hair above her ear and allowed his fingers to linger on her silken strands, which shimmered like liquid gold in the soft glow of the moon.

"Would you really have gone to your room and worked half the night?" he asked, his voice deep timbred, his question totally unexpected. "If Faye hadn't suggested we walk out here, would you be poring over computer print-outs right now?"

Shrugging, Abby stepped out onto the tiled colonnade, where classic simplicity was accented by potted shrubs and small ornamental trees. Discomfited by Joel's question, because she knew what the truthful answer should be, she attempted to qualify her response. "I don't think you can say I'd be 'poring over' anything. I might be glancing at some pertinent data, hoping to come up with some additional ideas for the presentation I'll be making."

"Why did you bring work with you to Fairfields in the first place?"

"I knew I wouldn't care to read or lounge around or swim at the beach every moment I was here, and I brought some work along to fill in any free time I might have."

"Most people are delighted to have some free time, but you sound as if you cringe at the very thought of it."

"I didn't mean to, because I enjoy free time as much as anyone else."

"Are you sure you don't just like to tell yourself that? Are you sure you don't plan each day so that every waking moment is occupied by some activity?"

"Whatever gave you that idea?" Abby asked, forcing a lightly amused laugh. "What is this anyway? Some kind of inquisition? Why all these strange questions?"

"Because you're a puzzle to me, Abby. I never know why you act the way you do, but I intend to find out," Joel stated, a sudden harder edge to his voice. Catching her arm when she automatically tried to turn away, he brought her back around to face him, pulling her several inches closer in the process. From his considerable height he looked down at her as if his shadowed eyes were trying to plumb the depths of hers for answers to his questions. His hand tightened almost imperceptibly around her arm. "For starters, you can tell me the reason you brought work with you on the first vacation you've probably taken

49

in two or three years. If it wasn't because you can't stand the thought of having free time on your hands, then why did you do it?"

"For heaven's sake. What's the big deal?" Abby exclaimed, self-defensive irritation masking the fleeting anguish that crossed over her delicate features. Though the moon shone down from behind Joel, putting him in shadow and shading his eyes, concealing whatever expression might have been in them, she met his unreadable gaze unwaveringly. "You and Faye act as if I committed a mortal sin by bringing my briefcase to Fairfields with me. It's only work that must be done eventually. What's wrong with doing some of it during my spare time here? I want this upcoming presentation to be as impressive as I can make it, because my career is important to me. And you can hardly fault me for that, Dr. Richmond, considering how important medicine is to you."

"Medicine is important to me, *very* important. But you'll notice I didn't bring any patients along on my vacation."

"Well, you have to admit that that would have been a lot more difficult than just bringing a briefcase, like I did. You can't really compare—"

"I didn't even bring any medical journals with me," Joel interrupted, touching a finger to Abby's lips, halting her rebuttal midsentence. "That means I'll have to do a great deal of catch-up reading when I get back to Charleston, but it will be worth it to have had two weeks away completely from what occupies my life every other day of the year."

"You have every right to feel that way. And I have every right not to."

"I couldn't agree more. And your bringing work with you isn't really the issue anyway—it's the way you use it as an escape from other people. And Faye thinks you have other ways of escaping. She told me what you brought

50

here with you—enough books to stock a small library, embroidery to finish, crochet needles, and yarn."

"I'd better warn you that Faye has an overactive imagination," Abby told him, trying to ignore the ache in her temples that seemed to be intensifying with every passing minute. "I really can't see what she finds so ominous about my reading or embroidering or crocheting."

"You have to admit all three are solitary occupations."

"Not necessarily. I can crochet or work on embroidery *and* be with other people at the same time, and even manage to hold my own in fairly intelligent conversations."

"Don't be flippant, Abby," Joel muttered, his hands moving swiftly to span her waist. "Resorting to flippancy during a serious discussion is just another means of escape. And none of your quick answers to my questions can change the fact that you secluded yourself in your room this afternoon and buried yourself in work, just to avoid talking to me about this morning."

Abby shook her head. "That's not true," she lied. "I didn't realize you thought there was anything to talk about."

"Damn it, when I asked you earlier what your problem was, I wanted answers. I still want some now. Exactly what is it you're running away from, Abby?"

She suddenly became very still and gazed up into his shadowed face.

"Tell me," he whispered coaxingly. "There's always been something reserved about you, something inside that you never shared with me even when we were practically living together. Tell me what it is. I need to understand."

"Why? Because you're a man of science and you can't resist a mystery? Your sister told me once you spent most of your childhood taking things apart to discover what made them tick." Abby swallowed convulsively but added defiantly, "Is that what you're trying to do with me? Trying to find out what makes me tick? I think that's exactly what you're trying to do. The problem is that you're wrong about me. I'm not the least bit mysterious. I am what I am."

"No, Abby, you're hiding something, and I plan to find out what," Joel promised, lowering his head as he spoke so that his words were a whispered warning in her ear. "If it takes forever, I'm going to make you tell me."

At that moment Abby longed to turn and run as far away from Joel as she possibly could, but she didn't. Although his warning filled her with dread, she showed no visible reaction to it. Instead, she withdrew behind the facade of a seemingly carefree smile, firmly extracted herself from his hold on her, and linked an arm around one of his with all the nonchalance she could muster. "Let's go back to the house. I'm really sleepy. All that swimming this morning is beginning to have its effect on me."

A few minutes later, after Joel and Abby returned to the living room together, she made her escape while pretending to suppress a yawn. Even as she walked across the hall toward the curving staircase, Abby could feel his eyes following her, boring into her back, and still issuing that warning promise he had made in the garden. Her throat was constricted, and she ran lightly up the steps despite the leaden heaviness in her legs. It was only after she was in the upper gallery and out of Joel's sight that she allowed her shoulders to droop. Staring blindly at the scrolled pattern of the carpet, she walked woodenly to her room, relieved to be able to close and lock the door behind her. She had escaped Joel once again, but only for the night. The following day he would still be there.

Biting down hard on her lower lip, she stripped off her clothes, pulled on a cool cotton nightgown, then dropped down across her bed, burying her face in her folded arms as weariness drained her of all energy. It was so ironic. The very secret that had compelled her to end everything

52

with Joel four months earlier now made her intriguingly mysterious to him; mysterious in a way he himself admitted he couldn't resist. She had become a puzzle he was determined to solve, and Abby wasn't sure she could withstand the tactics he might employ to achieve his objective. She couldn't tell him the truth about herself, and it would be sheer torment for her if he kept his promise and tried everything in his power to persuade her to tell him. She took a deep, shuddering breath. Her explicit curse was muffled in the crook of one arm. She didn't want to go through torture like that. Maybe it would be wise to just go back to Charleston. . . .

CHAPTER THREE

Two nights later Abby had still not returned to Charleston, having decided running from Joel would solve nothing at all. If anything, a hasty retreat by her might make her appear even more intriguing to him. And since he too would soon go back to Charleston . . . Well, she drew the line at moving away from the city she loved to escape him. No, it would be wiser in the long run to stick it out there at Fairfields, hoping Joel would realize that he had been wrong about her, that she was hiding nothing, and that there was really no mystique about her. After all, no one else, except Faye, considered her the least bit mysterious. She had never given anyone reason to. Because she had never allowed herself to dwell on her problem and because she truly enjoyed the work she did and the life she lived, no one she knew could ever imagine she had any troubles whatsoever. Perhaps Joel and Faye were simply too perceptive. Or perhaps, with Faye's overactive imagination influencing him, Joel was merely exaggerating the significance of Abby's occasional desire for solitude. He was really only guessing that she was hiding something from him, and correct as that supposition was, a guess was not

a strong conviction, and only minutes after first considering a retreat to Charleston, Abby had decided to stay at
Fairfields and convince Joel that he was totally mistaken
about her.

Then, after two days had passed, she was not at all sure
she had succeeded in convincing him of that. With Faye's
inimitable and unabashed encouragement, Joel deliberately spent almost all his time with Abby, challenging her to
impromptu tennis matches, taking her on horseback rides
that inevitably led to a couple of relaxing hours on the
beach, and spending the evenings in her company as if
there were nothing else he preferred to do. At first Abby
hadn't resisted spending time with him because she imagined she would only heighten his suspicions about her if
she did, but that consideration didn't last long. Joel was
simply fun to be with, and she felt increasingly and involuntarily drawn to his personable masculine charm. If
he had demanded anything of her, she might have been
able to make herself avoid him, but he demanded nothing.
Whenever he touched her, the touch was either casual or
accidental, and he had made no attempt to kiss her since
their morning on the beach. Abby's problem was that she
often looked up and found him watching her as if he
wanted to kiss her, and each time he didn't even make the
attempt she felt her already frazzled nerves being
stretched a little tauter. She had almost reached the point
where she wished he would kiss her simply so she could
prove that she could rebuff him.

"Idiot, you'd better hope he lets well enough alone," she
told her reflection in the vanity mirror as she sat in her
nightgown, brushing her hair. With a disgruntled sigh, she
laid the hairbrush down, glanced at her bed, and realized
that although it was nearly midnight, she was too restless
to go to sleep. Deciding she might as well get some work
done, she withdrew a folder from her briefcase, on the
floor beside the vanity, and opened it. No more than five

minutes later she slapped the folder shut with a muffled expletive of disgust. She couldn't concentrate at all. Even the upcoming presentation, which could be a major stepping-stone in her career, failed to hold her interest that night, and she found she could not sit still. She got up, padded barefoot across the room, and paused before a framed etching of Fairfields that a friend of Faye's had done. Delicate lines and shading strokes blurred to indistinction before eyes that weren't really seeing, and finally Abby moved away from the etching and walked slowly across her room. In a minute she wandered back again, wondering why she didn't feel the least bit sleepy.

Suddenly, out of the corner of her eye, she caught sight of a slight movement outside her partially opened French doors. She turned quickly to see what it was and her pulse began to throb wildly when Joel pushed the doors open wider and stepped into her room. Faye had given the two of them rooms that opened onto a common balcony—another of her matchmaking ploys—but, until that night, Joel had never acted as if he even realized that he had been afforded such easy access to Abby's room. Then he was nonchalantly strolling in there, giving her an almost boyishly charming smile.

"I stepped out on the balcony for some fresh air and saw you moving around in here. Thought you wouldn't mind some company," he explained carelessly. "It's obvious you aren't sleepy."

"Not very," she admitted, her voice steady despite the frantic palpitations of her heart, which she was trying to no avail to control. Joel's attire, tan pajama pants slung low on his lean hips, suddenly reminded her of the diaphanousness of the fine lawn nightgown she wore, and she reached for her lightweight cotton duster and put it on. Faint pink color mantled her cheeks when Joel's amused expression seemed to indicate that he thought her modesty unnecessary, since he had seen her often enough without

56

any clothes on at all. Still, she gathered the duster closely around her body and immediately felt more in control of the situation.

"Since I'm not sleepy either," Joel went on, "I figured we might as well be awake together."

"Sure, why not." Abby indicated with a gesture of her hand the easy chair near her bed. "Have a seat, and we can talk a little while, if you like."

After Abby settled on the edge of the bed, Joel sat down too, the picture of casual yet somehow dangerous masculinity as he crossed his long outstretched legs at the ankle and leaned back comfortably in the chair.

Abby's gaze lingered for a long moment on the bronze glow of his bare chest in the light, then she lifted her eyes to his face and gave him a faint smile as she folded her hands primly in her lap. "Well, it is rather balmy tonight, isn't it? I suppose that's why we aren't sleepy."

"Could be," Joel agreed with a nod of his head.

"It might get cooler, though; looks like some of the clouds are breaking up. Don't you think? When I looked out a few minutes ago, I saw a few stars, and earlier I . . . wasn't able to see . . . any . . ." Abby's voice trailed off with her sudden realization that she was actually sitting in her bedroom late at night with her former lover and discussing the *weather,* of all things. How utterly asinine! Shifting uneasily on the edge of the bed, she tucked the hems of both her gown and duster tightly around her knees and miraculously thought of a topic at least a bit more interesting to talk about. "Oh, I've been meaning to ask you if Nell decided to retire from nursing or not."

"Definitely not. Oh, she still talks all the time about retiring, but I don't imagine she will until she has absolutely no other choice. I hope not; the clinic's pediatric department wouldn't be the same without her." Joel's fond smile became a low chuckle. "Besides, she disciplines interns more effectively than any other head nurse I've

57

ever known. After one of her sermons, an intern will do almost anything to win her approval again. I heard her dressing down one the other day for not answering his page as quickly as she thought he should have." Joel's voice raised in pitch to a squeaky falsetto as he quoted his favorite nurse. " 'You surely are a disappointment to me, young man, and I did have such high hopes for your future in medicine. But never mind that you *were* one of my favorite interns. If you dawdle around and wait this long to answer a page ever again, I'll recommend to Dr. Richmond that you be assigned to bedpan duty for a week. And we'll just see how you cotton to that.' "

Abby's uneasiness was forgotten and, for a few moments, she couldn't stop laughing. "You sound just like Nell" she was able to say at last, though she was still chuckling merrily. "Joel, you're so funny. Did you know you probably could have made a fortune as an impressionist if you hadn't decided to be a doctor?"

"I love to hear you laugh" was Joel's abruptly solemn response as he rose to his feet. His narrowed gaze never left Abby's face as, with one stride, he eliminated the distance between the chair and the bed. "I'll have to try to be funny more often, just to hear you."

Abby's laughter ceased with her sharp intake of breath and she stood slowly, though her legs were weak and unsteady. In a split second the atmosphere in her room had altered considerably and then seemed electrically charged. Her breathing quickened, and it was almost reflex action that made her try to sidestep Joel when he moved directly in front of her. And when he caught hold of her arms and wouldn't allow her to pass, she actually felt dizzy for an instant. She had to close her eyes momentarily to regain her equilibrium, then she opened them again, murmuring, "Maybe you better go now, Joel."

"No, not yet, love," he whispered, lowering his dark head. "Not until I do this." His warm lips barely brushed across hers. He drew away slightly. "And this." His lips brushed hers again.

When he drew away once more, Abby moaned inwardly. For two days she had been waiting for Joel to kiss her, but not like this, never like this. Because she had expected him to take possession of her mouth with a demand she could have resisted, she had not been prepared for the delicate stroking kisses that, to her everlasting shame, only made her hungry for more. She began to tremble as Joel's lips teased the soft full shape of hers again and again and again, until she felt she would cry out if he didn't stop and *knew* she would if he did.

He didn't. The pressure of his mouth on hers increased ever so slightly. He nibbled her tender lips and his last kiss became a long, continuing arousal of her senses. Abby's clenched hands moved to his chest, and while her fingers gradually spread open to move in soft caresses, Joel sought the snaps of her duster and slowly pulled them open one by one.

"No," she breathed weakly against his firm lips when he removed her arms from the sleeves and allowed the duster to fall to the floor around her feet. "Joel, don't."

"Don't what, Abby?" he questioned, gently imprisoning her hand in his while he stepped back a short distance. His gaze wandered over her, his eyes warm and glowing with a secret illumination. "Don't stop undressing you? Or don't look at you like this? Did you know I can see right through that gown in this light? You don't have anything on underneath it, do you?"

The sensual roughness of his voice was Abby's undoing. She felt set adrift in a dreamworld where she could control neither her feelings nor her responses. She could only long for him to touch her again, and when he did, her breath caught audibly. Through her lashes she watched with fascination as Joel's lean fingers outlined the tips of her breasts, just visible through the sheer gown. Waves of heat coursed through her veins, and when Joel stopped touching her, love made her step toward him.

Joel took her hands, pressed them against his body, then cupped her face in his own. He leaned down. His lips grazed the sweep of her eyebrows, then each temple, then the hollow beneath one ear. When he nibbled the tender fleshy lobe and a tremor ran through her, he moved nearer, and at long last his mouth covered hers once more.

Joel's kiss was seductively gentle, and Abby's senses were already reeling. It was glorious being secluded in this room with him, as if everything and everyone in the outside world had ceased to exist. Her fingers moved in slow circles over his chest, then began to trace the prominent contours. Muscle contracted beneath her fingertips, became powerfully taut in masculine response. The hardening of Joel's lips and the arms that tightened around her were echoed throughout the length of his lithe body. His urgently deepening kiss ravished her soft lips with slightly twisting pressure. They parted wider, and as his teeth closed lightly on the fuller lower curve, playing with it, tasting it, thrill after thrill of sexual excitement rushed through Abby, weakening her lower limbs. She wrapped her arms eagerly around the back of Joel's neck, entwining her slim fingers in his hair. He bore part of her weight now, which eased her trembling legs and brought her so close to him, she could feel the strong, fierce beating of his heart against her breasts. Each kiss led immediately to another, every one lengthening and becoming a more intense and quickening seduction. Abby's sweet lips rubbed his, teasing, tantalizing, exploring, before parting like a slowly opening flower to invite a rougher taking of her mouth.

As she deliberately heightened his desire he complied, clasping the back of her head in one hand, holding her fast as he proceeded to demonstrate how passionate his kisses could be. Hard marauding lips took complete possession of hers, hungrily plundering their tender sweetness and taking as an added prize the ardency of her response as she returned the kisses and feverishly pressed closer and closer to him. Her breath mingled hotly with his, and Abby felt so much a part of him that she sighed sadly when his lips left her own several minutes later. Drowsy blue eyes flickered open and encountered the smoldering dark glow in the often unfathomable depths of his.

Joel's slow smile softened his hard features when he whispered, "Tonight you don't taste at all like salt."

"You don't either."

"You taste like . . . hmm, I can't seem to identify exactly what you do taste like. Maybe another sample . . ." His dark head came down. His lips played lazily over hers. The tip of his tongue flicked over their soft texture until they parted. The kiss that followed lingered gently before Joel raised his head again. "You don't taste like honey. Or wine," he decided, his brows knitted as he pretended to concentrate. "Maybe some combination of the two." With awesome swiftness he kissed her again, then smiled triumphantly. "I have it. You taste like ambrosia."

Abby laughed at him. "Ambrosia was a mythical drink of the gods. How could you possibly know what it tastes like?"

He shrugged. "It must taste like you. You're delicious. And what do I taste like, if not salt?"

Captivated by the game, Abby smiled secretively, stretched up, and sought firmly chiseled lips. Her kiss lingered too before she nodded with satisfaction. "You taste like mint. No, to be precise, a mint julep."

"Intoxicating?"

"Oh, a little."

"Enough to loosen inhibitions?" he inquired, giving her no chance to answer as he lowered himself onto the wide bed and drew her down with him. Turning over onto his side toward her, he trailed one hand slowly up along her silken thigh, followed her curving hip to her waist, and continued higher to her rising breasts. His fingers slipped beneath one strap of her nightgown, then the other, pushing both off her shoulders until they draped loosely around her upper arms. Smiling indulgently at Abby's sudden stillness, he lifted her head slightly to brush her hair up and back. Fanning out in golden waves on the pillow, it framed her face but completely bared her shoulders to the probing kisses that followed.

Sparks of fire danced on Abby's skin everywhere he placed a lingering kiss. She had to touch him, too; feeling the texture of his copper skin became a physical necessity to her. One arm slipped up across his shoulders while she explored with light fingertips the planes and contours of his face. Abby's eyes closed and her lips parted with the quick breath she had to take when Joel's kisses traveled lower and moved evocatively over the feminine flesh visible above the top of her gown.

"*Abby,*" he whispered with heated demand while swiftly pulling the nightgown down and exposing her breasts. Heavy-lidded dark eyes watched the rapid rise and fall and admired frankly the porcelain, rose-tipped skin, which was stretched taut.

His lingering appraisal created such a feeling of utter vulnerability in Abby that her heart began to thud with trip-hammer rapidity. With a knowing smile, Joel drew the hard edge of one hand along the hollow between her breasts and around until the full weight of one breast rested against his palm. The ball of his thumb glided over and around the peak until it rose to a firm, sensitized nubble for questing fingers to tease. Fire that was blazing within her rose to the surface of her skin and radiated compelling heat. Joel's hand moved to her other breast, his fingers pressing into and stroking her resilient flesh. Abby moaned softly and caressed the smooth expanse of his back. When his lips took swift, insistent possession of hers once again, she wrapped her arms around him and protested faintly when his hand curved over one hipbone suddenly held her down against the bed.

Joel's mouth left her own to seek first one breast, then the other, closing with a firm, pulling pressure around her throbbing, tumescent peaks. He flicked the tip of his tongue over her hot skin, playing lazily with the sweet nubbles of flesh until Abby was dizzy with desire for him. An empty aching opened deep inside her and her long legs tangled with the muscular length of his, their slow, sensuous movement arousing him to an iron hardness that surged powerfully against one silken thigh.

Joel groaned softly, kissed her ravenously again and again, but did not take what Abby needed very badly to give. Never a man to rush lovemaking, he continued to caress her and respond to her caresses, arousing her need for him to a fever pitch. In the process, he also aroused memories. This slow, thorough seduction was so reminiscent of the first time they had made love that Abby began to feel she was reliving that moment. It was almost as if she were surrendering herself to Joel for the first time. And that feeling in itself made it practically impossible for her to heed the frantic warnings her brain was trying to give her. At that moment her love for Joel was too overpowering for her to heed anything. She ached to know his intimately possessing strength again; she longed to give him the physical satisfaction he now so obviously needed. She didn't want to deny him that. She didn't want to deny him anything.

Now the warning signals were fading in and out of her mind, weaker each time they faded in. Joel's irresistible touches and kisses had brought her to the verge of total surrender . . . yet, some tattered remnants of her sanity caused her to tense when he slipped a hand gently between her thighs. Abby trembled violently, and when a sound reminiscent of a half sob escaped her lips, Joel released her

63

reluctantly, shaking his head as he sat up on the edge of the bed beside her.

"You're not ready for this yet," he said softly when she opened surprised eyes to look up at him. After raking long fingers through his hair, he pulled one side of the quilted coverlet over her bared breasts, then touched her face lightly, giving her a faint indulgent smile. "You're not ready yet, but you soon will be, and I can wait until you are."

Incapable of uttering any response, Abby watched as he strode resolutely to the French doors and onto the balcony and out of her sight. He was gone, and she closed her eyes, turned her face into the pillow, and breathed a long tremulous sigh. She should have been greatly relieved that common sense had finally proven stronger than her traitorous body, yet the relief she felt was only partial and not at all gratifying. Her physical being still ached for the satisfaction only Joel could provide, and for a crazy moment she actually considered going to him, then tried to push that insane thought right out of her mind. When it refused to be banished completely from consciousness, she pressed her fingertips against her hot aching eyes. She wasn't sure how much longer she could withstand the emotional roller coaster ride before she either ran back to Charleston or surrendered to Joel and her own rising need to give him all her love, just one more time.

CHAPTER FOUR

After rising early the next morning, Abby bathed and dressed in denim cut-offs and her most comfortable T-shirt, then hurried downstairs to begin what she knew would be a hectic day. That evening the Howards were holding Faye's third annual Magnolia Ball, Abby's first, and she was looking forward to it. In the main hall she smiled as she followed Faye, who had suddenly dashed out of the dining room and into the kitchen, where she dialed the caterer and commenced an animated, fairly one-sided conversation. Somewhat breathless when she replaced the receiver several minutes later, Faye smiled ruefully while watching Abby pour a cup of steaming coffee for each of them.

"Oh, I do need that. Thanks," she said, taking a long swallow. "I have *so* much to do today that I'm not a bit sure how I'll manage to get it all done."

Abby helped. By lending her expertise at flower arranging, she relieved Faye of that time-consuming responsibility. For much of the morning Abby carefully gathered flowers from the gardens and placed them in large cans filled with water until the sun-room, where she was working, was crowded with blooms. Surrounded by early June's bounty of scarlet gladioli, snowy oleander, a number of the loveliest magnolia blossoms still remaining on the trees, plus an incredible variety of other flowers in a myriad of colors, Abby worked contentedly. Humming softly, she filled vase after vase with artistically arranged bouquets of emerald-green ferns and vibrantly hued blooms. It was nearly eleven thirty before she had finished placing the arrangements strategically in the main hall, all the downstairs rooms, and many of the rooms upstairs.

On her way back to the sun-room to clean up the cut stems and discarded leaves she had left there, she found Faye and Joel in the main hall, standing in front of the table where she had placed the largest arrangement, which consisted of an antique silver bowl filled predominantly with waxy magnolia blossoms, some scarlet rosebuds for accent, and the greenest, most perfect fern fronds she had found.

"Oh, Abby, it's just lovely. I could just stand here all day and look at it. You've done such a beautiful job with all the flowers," Faye exclaimed sincerely. "I may make you my official flower arranger. Joel, don't you think I ought to?"

Darkening eyes swept slowly upward from Abby's bare feet, over the cut-offs and now smudged T-shirt to her appealingly small face and the golden disarray of hair that framed it. He nodded at last, in answer to Faye's question, then said softly, "These really are beautiful arrangements, Abby."

After inclining her head with a pleased smile to acknowledge the obviously genuine compliment, Abby hooked her thumbs in the back pockets of her cut-offs and grinned mischievously, her own gaze taking in Joel's grass-stained khaki pants and cream-colored polo shirt. "And obviously, while we've been busy in the house, you were drafted to do yard work."

"How could you tell?" was his wry retort, accompanied by an answering grin. "I've been with the gardener all morning, helping trim the grass around the hedge by the gate. And right now I could use a shower."

"After you've had one, would you take Abby to pick up our dresses from the seamstress? They won't get so wrinkled in your car, since it's roomier than hers is," Faye spoke up, trying to pretend she hadn't just cooked up another excuse to bring the two of them together alone again. But when Joel readily agreed to her request, a quick satisfied smile betrayed her.

Abby had a shower too, slipped into a sundress, and, twenty minutes later, met Joel in the main hall. He had already driven his pearl-white Volvo GLE around to the front of the house, and they left immediately, Abby directing him. Back along Bohicket Road about a mile, Essie Taylor's small clapboard house was easy to find. A tall, rather regal-looking woman in her late thirties, Essie welcomed them into her parlor, served iced tea in tall glasses with sprigs of fresh mint, then left them for a moment. When she returned with two dresses, the apple-green taffeta for Faye, the indigo-blue with ecru lace for Abby, Abby's eyes widened.

"Oh, Essie, they're both beautiful! Perfect!" she said softly, rather in awe of the woman's talent as she got up to take a closer look. She glanced back at Joel. "Can you believe she made these with nothing to go by except drawings of two gowns from the mid-eighteen hundreds?"

He was impressed and smiled at Essie. "You do very fine work, Mrs. Taylor."

"Thank you, Dr. Richmond," she replied, while examining Abby with a practiced eye. "You've lost a bit of weight, but not very much, I hope, or the dress won't fit proper."

"Only a couple of pounds. Three at the most."

"Ought to be all right, then."

As Essie spoke a back bedroom door opened, and a lovely little girl no older than two stepped into the parlor. In a beam of sunlight that shone through a window, her ebony skin looked soft as fine velvet, but she stared at Abby and Joel with a typical toddler's suspicion as she walked to her mother and clutched a handful of skirt. Plopping a thumb in her mouth, she leaned against Essie's legs and softly whimpered.

"Anything wrong, Mrs. Taylor?" Joel asked immediately, his attention exclusively on the child.

"Well, yes. I think maybe Mary's got a little something. She's been fretful all morning. Didn't even want to play with her brothers and sisters," Essie told him, a worried frown now creasing her brow. "And about an hour ago she started pulling on her left ear, so we're taking the bus into Charleston this afternoon, and I'm carrying her to the clinic."

"Maybe I can save you the trip," Joel offered, leaning forward on the sofa to lightly touch Mary's hand. When he beckoned her to him with a smile, she amazingly went. He glanced up. "Abby, my bag is in the back of the car. Get it for me, please."

By the time Abby returned to the parlor and handed Joel the black bag, he had won Mary over completely. She sat as quiet as a mouse on his lap while he examined her nose and throat in addition to both ears. He checked her heart and lungs with a stethoscope, smiling when she giggled each time he moved the metal disk across her chest.

"She has a little infection in the left ear," he announced at the end of the examination. "I'll write a prescription for penicillin. It'll be a pink liquid that will smell like candy but won't taste nearly as nice. She won't want to take it, but she has to, all of it, even after the ear stops hurting. Okay?"

Essie nodded. "Doctor, I sure do appreciate this. It's

such a long bus ride to Charleston, and with a child fretting with an earache . . . Well, I'll ask my neighbor to go to the drugstore for this medicine right away. And, naturally, I want to pay you for—"

"Speaking of paying, I owe you for the dresses," Abby interceded, diverting Essie's thoughts, because she could see Joel didn't want to charge for the examination. She rummaged through her purse, then brought out the check Faye had written for her gown and cash for her own. She put the money down on a side table, gingerly cradled the crushable dresses in her arms, and, while Joel stood to hand Mary to her mother, devised an excuse for their hasty departure.

Abby and Joel made it to the car but hadn't gotten in when Essie hurried out her front door, worn wallet in her hand, and called after them, "Wait. I never did pay you, Dr. Richmond."

"I'll send you a bill," he called back, though he knew he wouldn't.

When the dresses had been tucked neatly into the car, they started back to Fairfields. During a brief silence Abby suddenly laughed aloud, and Joel's brows lifted questioningly as he looked her way.

"Something just occurred to me," she explained. "You didn't bring your patients with you on vacation, but you certainly don't mind picking up new ones anywhere you can. I guess you really didn't leave *all* thoughts of work back in Charleston after all, did you?"

"Point taken," he responded with a smile that was somewhat sheepish and very endearing. He lifted his shoulders in a resigned shrug. "The truth is, I never could resist a kid."

The glimmer of amusement slowly faded from Abby's eyes. "I know," she said softly, then turned her head to stare at nothing out her window.

The busy afternoon swept by, and once the ball began

that evening, time flew. When Abby at last left the dance floor in search of much-needed liquid refreshment, she could hardly believe it was close to eleven. She had been dancing nonstop for nearly three hours. Little wonder her feet were beginning to ache. But the ball was a tremendous success, and she was truly enjoying it. Sipping fruit punch compromised by rum, she looked out over the living room, cleared of furniture, and watched the shadowy reflections of the swirling dancers in the polished surface of the hard-wood floor. In their finery, they seemed to recapture a past that had been far more elegant that the present was, and surveying the pretty scene had an almost mesmerizing effect. Abby glanced around, seeking out Joel and locating him on the opposite side of the room, where a statuesque blonde danced closely with him. Abby smiled faintly. As she herself hadn't lacked dance partners all evening, nei-ther had he. Everytime she had caught a glimpse of him, he had been dancing with a different young woman or surrounded by several. Abby had only danced with him twice, but with so many people around it wasn't surprising that she had seen so little of him throughout the evening. Even then she lost sight of him again as he moved among the dancers.

Not ready yet to risk having her toes trod upon again, Abby left her unfinished punch on an empty silver tray and strolled out onto the veranda. Garlands of magnolia blooms festooned the wrought-iron railing, perfuming the blessedly cooler night air. Gazing out across the sweeping lawn, she leaned against a white pillar and smiled au-tomatically when a hand touched her arm.

"Oh, Joel, hi," she murmured, her heart rate accelerat-ing slightly as it always did when she saw him. "Getting some fresh air, too?"

"Is that what you came out here for?" he asked, answer-ing her question with a question. "Why aren't you danc-ing?"

"Oh, *please*," she groaned with a wry smile. "Dancing is all I've been doing. My feet needed a break."

"Actually, mine did, too."

"It's been a long day."

"You sound a little tired," he said, leaning nearer, one hand placed against the pillar above her head while the other played idly with the end of the ecru sash that accentuated her narrow waist. "Are you?"

"A bit tired, I guess. The fresh air has revived me. It's sort of close inside with all those people."

"Um-hum." He moved closer still and gently touched her face. "You look exquisite in that dress."

Smiling, Abby laid her hands against the fitted bodice. "It is beautiful, isn't it."

"It's beautiful, yes, but *you're* exquisite," he corrected her huskily. His hands covered hers, his thumbs slowly brushing over the upsweeping curves of her breasts as he pulled her to him and bent down to caress her lips with the warm hardness of his. He lifted his head slightly to capture and hold her bemused gaze. His thumbs continued their disruptive exploration of rounded flesh, and he whispered, "We don't have to stay here, Abby. We could drive somewhere. I left the car near the gate in case of an emergency—an old doctor's habit."

"You're not an *old* doctor," she whispered back, her smile tremulous, her heart pounding now.

"I have the old habits, though. But never mind that." He slipped his hands beneath hers, his palms warming her skin through the bodice. "Will you go for a drive with me?"

Abby couldn't give an answer as she allowed her gaze to wander over him. He looked incredibly dashing in close-fitting black trousers that emphasized the muscles of his long legs. He also wore a black coat that was tapered at his waist, flaring out over his lean hips, and was made less severe by the snowy pleated shirt beneath it. His high

71

collar's stark whiteness deepened the bronze tan of his neck and face, and as her eyes drifted up to meet his, Abby felt a desperate need rush through her, a need to touch him. As he stood in the light spilling from the windows she could see his face as clearly as she could in daylight, yet his expression was unreadable, and she was unable to look away.

"Well, Abby," he prompted when her silence extended several long seconds. "Will you go with me?"

"Where?" she breathed.

"To the beach," he murmured, possessive hands skimming around her waist. "We're both tired of dancing, tired of the crush of people, so come with me now."

"But, Faye . . ." Abby protested, holding back slightly even as his arm across the small of her back impelled her down onto the first step of the broad veranda stairs. "I can't just leave. Faye will worry if I simply disappear."

"She'll notice I'm not here, either. She won't worry, knowing we're together. Now, let's go before someone waylays us out here," Joel coaxed, lowering his dark head to seek one corner of her mouth, then the other, again and again, whispering between the tantalizing kisses, "You do *want* to go with me, don't you, Abby?"

Perhaps it was the magical effect of a night from the past, combined with his nearness and his insistence, that made excitement rush through her veins in tidal waves, excitement that made her feel vitally alive and unafraid. "Yes, I want to come with you," she admitted, her voice hushed as she awaited his kiss. Her delicately curved lips parted beneath the swiftly increasing pressure of his. With an urgent murmuring of her name, he drew her into the shadows at the foot of the stairs. His hands molded her hips, brought her tight against him, and his obvious passion caused her own to erupt in a fiery blaze that seared within. Emitting a low groan, Joel released her mouth. When he drew her close to his side, a bare shapely arm slipped around his waist. Abby's head nuzzled the hollow of his shoulder as they walked together across the lawn toward the driveway. She glanced up at the star-studded sky, but that made her head swim. Everything suddenly seemed unreal, dreamlike. Yet, in the deepest recesses of her mind, she knew that someday, maybe tomorrow, she might realize that tonight had been a terrible mistake. She might . . . But, right now, she didn't really care if she ever did.

CHAPTER FIVE

Joel parked the car where the lane ended at the beach house. He got out and went around to Abby's side to help her with her voluminous skirt, billowed out by a crinoline underneath. As if she were accustomed to wearing such clothing every day of the week, she turned with smooth grace in the seat and stepped out onto the lane beside him. To her surprise, when Joel took her hand in his, he led her neither to the bungalow nor the beach. Instead, he followed a path that curved with the crescent of sand that edged the shoreline until they came upon the pier jutting out into the water. Near the end of the sturdy wooden structure, in Fairfields's private dock, *Sea Nymph*, the Howard's forty-foot sloop, bobbed gently in her berth.

"Come aboard." Joel spoke for the first time since leaving the car. Stepping down onto the gleaming deck, he reached up, gripped Abby's waist in strong, capable hands, and easily swung her down beside him. "A perfect night to take her out, isn't it?"

Her head tilted questioningly to one side. "We're not exactly dressed for sailing, are we?"

He agreed. "But, under power, we can cruise around to the cove and drop anchor there."

Abby's hands, drifting up to rest almost weightlessly against his chest, shook slightly in direct relation to the abrupt frantic pounding of her heart. She knew precisely why Joel wanted to take her to such a secluded spot. She could have refused to go but didn't. The tip of her tongue came out to moisten suddenly dry lips, yet she smiled. "The cove sounds nice. It's very quiet there."

"And perfectly private," he added provocatively, releasing her with discernible reluctance. Turning, he stepped down into the open topside cockpit, reached into his pocket, and fished out a key that he slipped into the ignition on the control panel.

Abby stepped down beside him. "I see you came prepared."

"Always the boy scout, that's me," Joel said, a note of teasing amusement in his low voice as he playfully tugged at a strand of her moon-gilded hair. With a flick of his wrist, he turned the key. Below, a nearly silent diesel engine purred to life. Leaving it to idle, he went to tie off all except the two forward lines. When he returned, he grazed one hand over Abby's left hip, his fingertips stroking the smooth silky texture of her dress as he inquired, "Think you can manage to cast off the forward dock lines, wearing that?"

With a nod, Abby left him and made her way forward, the hem of her wide bell-shaped skirt swishing against the cabin portholes on one side and the bow railing on the other. Kneeling on the scrupulously clean gunwale, she stretched to reach the lines and accomplished her task. Smoothly reversing, Joel eased *Sea Nymph* out of the berth, and by the time Abby rejoined him in the cockpit, they had cleared the dock. As Joel picked up speed and headed toward deeper water to follow the shoreline south a short distance to the cove, a salt-scented wind lifted

Abby's hair, cooling her warm nape. Aware of Joel's gaze, she smiled up at him and nuzzled her cheek against the hard knuckles he tenderly brushed across her satin-smooth skin. Her eyes briefly closed, and she released a deeply drawn breath in a shuddery silent sigh as his touch lingered, warming her, relaxing her, seducing her.

Five minutes later Joel cut the engine and dropped anchor in the cove, a cul-de-sac bound on three sides by rock-strewn shore. *Sea Nymph* rocked gently in the waves that washed in through the wide cove entrance, beyond which stretched the open sea. On deck, at the stern railing, Abby looked out, fascinated by the constant undulating motion of the water. Moonlight shimmered like silver on the rippling surface, and phosphorescent spray danced up, then showered down in magical light displays as eternally successive waves were dashed to foam against the low wall of rocks encompassing three quarters of the cove. Beneath a canopy of velvet sky bejeweled with twinkling stars, Abby felt a sense of oneness with the ocean that she had never before experienced. As she musingly considered how easy it might be for her to become a true child of nature, Joel joined her at the railing. When his arm slipped across her shoulders, the sensations his touch evoked seemed as natural in the basic scheme of things as the sea below her and the sky above. Enchanted, suddenly freed of even the slightest inhibition, she gave in to a very earthy compulsion to touch and lifted a hand to play with the long fingers lightly curved around her upper arm.

"I'm glad we came here," she said after several moments. "Anchor all secure?"

"Snagged between some rocks, if I'm not mistaken," Joel told her. "We may have trouble raising it later."

Abby looked up at him. "And if we can't unsnag it, would we be stranded here? For days maybe?"

Amusement tugged upward at the corners of Joel's

mouth. "Well, now, I suppose that's within the realm of possibility. And if we were stranded?"

"I think I'd like it very much." In the circle of his arm, Abby turned to face him. "I could make us coffee now, if you'd like some," she offered, not as a subterfuge but as a natural expression of an inbred courtesy. "I'm sure I can find everything I need down in the galley. Or maybe you'd rather have a brandy? I would."

"I'll get us both one."

Leaving her, Joel went below and returned shortly with two small crystal snifters into which he had poured the barest amounts of the crimson liquid. Abby took small savoring sips of the brandy he gave her and gazed in silence out toward the open ocean. Much of her brandy remained when, fifteen minutes later, Joel resolutely slipped the stem of the snifter from between her fingers and placed the unfinished drink with his on a small round table bolted to the deck.

Straightening, he caught her hands in his and slowly pulled her close, drawing her arms around him. Gathering her hair back, he wound it around one hand and very gently tilted her face up. His head lowered, he traced kisses along the graceful curve of her ivory neck and across her creamy shoulders. The tip of his tongue tasted her skin, and the kisses moved lower, and his warm breath was a caress in the scented hollow between her breasts. Although the off-the-shoulder neckline made the gown décolleté, what it exposed of Abby wasn't enough for Joel. He eased the dress farther down her arms. The bodice dropped a bit, and Abby's breath caught as his teeth closed on the fabric, pulling it down until the generously full slopes of the tops of her breasts were bared to his gaze and touch. And touch he did, with light fingertips first, feathering her soft pliant flesh, readying Abby for the more inflaming exploration conducted by his lips.

"*Joel,*" Abby murmured, massaging the corded muscles

77

of his shoulders and back while his breath fanned her deep inviting cleavage. His mouth on her now conveyed more impassioned demand, his vital heat penetrating her skin, causing a shaft of fire to flare deep inside her. She unbuttoned his coat and slipped her hands inside, playing them over his chest, kneading his lean sides, then cupping the strong column of his neck. Her fingertip traced the edge of his ear. With an urgent whisper, she lifted his head and grazed her parted lips over the carved shape of his, satisfied only when his arms tightened roughly around her and his hard mouth ravished her own with deepening kisses.

"God, I've missed you!" Joel at last uttered hoarsely.

And knowing he meant it, Abby was hopelessly lost. She allowed him to take her hands and draw her down the private companionway that led to the stateroom below. Cupping her jaw, he kissed her much more gently than he had only moments earlier and reached behind her to flip a switch. A small wall-mounted lamp came on, dimly illuminating the teak-paneled cabin and catching the soft glimmer in Abby's lambent aqua eyes as she looked up at Joel's sunbrowned face. The expression that lay over his chiseled features gentled as he looked back at her, and the glint of desire in the black depths of his eyes was tempered by a sudden tenderness.

Overflowing with love for him, Abby stroked his dark hair when he went down on one knee before her to lift one foot, then the other, removing her low-heeled slippers. He set them aside, beneath a chair, rose up, and touched her face. Her soft smile betrayed a certain feeling of vulnerability and she half turned away, looking around the cabin, taking in the wide captain's bed with drawers built in underneath, covered with a richly embroidered red-and-gold spread.

Abby heard Joel move behind her. His hands encircled her waist, his fingers spreading open possessively across her abdomen and pressing her back against him. He brushed her shining hair over one shoulder, then his arms were around her again, his hands cupping her breasts, his palms weighing their ripe fullness. When a tremor ran lightly through Abby, Joel leaned down to kiss the sweet skin of her exposed nape. She started to turn to him, but he didn't allow it.

"Wait," he commanded softly, touching her shoulders before his fingers sought the first in a row of tiny buttons that marched down the low-cut basque and continued into the skirt over the gentle curve of her hips. He undid one, then the next.

Progress was made slowly. Even his dexterous fingers were uncharacteristically unsteady now and he was unable to unfasten quickly such diminutive buttons. After several moments, he pressed a kiss between her shoulder blades and murmured against her skin, "God, what I wouldn't do for a zipper right now."

"They didn't have zippers in the mid-eighteen hundreds," Abby explained, more than a hint of amusement in her voice. "The buttons are for authenticity."

"Damn authenticity," Joel murmured, then, with a swift little jerk, opened the basque and the placket of the skirt.

Abby gasped as a rush of air struck her bare back and the small cloth-covered buttons scattered soundlessly around her on the plush carpet. But laughter bubbled up as she halfheartedly chided, "Oh, Joel, think of the time it took Essie to sew all those on."

"If she knew how I feel right now, she'd forgive me, I'm sure" was his reply while he swept the dress off Abby's arms, then let it fall with a silky whisper down around her feet. At his expectant gaze she stepped out of it, and he picked it up to lay it across a chair. His narrowed eyes roamed, surveyed her loveliness, then met the vivid blue of hers, where amusement had now been replaced by feelings much more profound. An almost indulgent smile moved his hard mouth. His gaze dropped to the crinoline that cascaded frothily down from waist to toe, its net fabric covering, but not totally concealing, her slender form outlined under it.

Joel reached out and undid the narrow band tied at the waist. The petticoat dropped with a rustling sound. Stockingless, her long lightly tanned legs left bare for comfort and coolness, Abby stood before him clad only in ivory lace-embellished panties and a matching strapless bra. Both were scanty modern articles of apparel and certainly at variance with the old-fashioned undergarment that had now settled in a cloud around her ankles. The incongruousness failed to capture Joel's notice, however. His thoughts seemed to be on far different matters as he stood motionless, looking at Abby.

She shivered but not from cold. She was too conscious of her state of undress, because Joel was still fully clothed, while only two skimpy scraps of cloth prevented her from being completely naked. She swallowed hard.

Almost if he had read her thoughts, Joel did not continue to undress her. Instead, he lifted her small hands to the intricately tied cravat around his neck. "Take it off," he urged. When she had obeyed, then unbuttoned his white shirt as well, he watched as her slightly trembling fingers pushed aside the fabric and ran with the lightness of kittens' feet across his bronze hair-roughened skin. He took her into his arms then, his hands on her back probing the delicate structure of bones and flesh, his fingertips sampling the alabaster-smooth texture of her skin.

Abby's arms wound around his neck and she went up on her toes, arching against him as they kissed. Her soft parted lips moved beneath the firmer shape of his, and the tip of her tongue met his as it flicked into her mouth.

"I *want* you, Abby," he muttered, his deep voice strained, his tone uneven. And with the words, he sought the back closure of her bra, unhooking it and slipping it off. The softness of her breasts yielded to the hardness of his chest when he pulled her tight against him once more. His lips found hers again in a breathtaking progression of lengthening consuming kisses. Abby ran her fingers through his clean hair, delighting in the feel of it, delighting in him. His superior strength and his obvious arousal caused a warming weakness to race through her limbs.

Joel felt her sway slightly in his embrace. He took her to the bed, threw back the covers, then lifted her in his arms to lay her down. Bending over her, he kissed her again as if he could never get his fill of her sweetness. Yet when she wound her arms around his waist and her hands on his broad back urged him down to her, he dragged himself away.

Lying there watching as he stripped off his shoes, socks, and trousers, Abby waited. The strangely magical night and the immeasurable depth of her love for him had taken hold of her, and rational thought was no longer possible. She could only feel . . . *experience* a true completeness because she was with him again. Released from the agonized longing for him that she had endured for weeks, she could feel that it must be right for them to be together there. Never in her life had she wanted anything more than she wanted to give to him and take what he would give. She ached for him.

Her eyes drifted over his magnificent virile body and issued an unmistakable invitation as he lay down on the bed. Propped on one elbow, he lay on his side and looked at her, visually exploring every inch, from the tips of her toes to the top of her head. Then his deeply tanned hand began a more disruptive exploration, sweeping over her ivory skin. He eased her onto her side to face him. With the backs of his fingers, he stroked her arm, the lines of her slender thigh and shapely calf, then his palm reversed the path his fingers had taken and came back up again. His hand reached her shoulder, slipped under her arm, and feathered down to cup the side of her breast, lingering warmly there before continuing to follow the alluring sweep of her waist and the gentle swell of her hip.

Abby's pulses raced. She lightly touched Joel's lips, her heart leaping when he suddenly caught a fingertip gently between his teeth. He nibbled tenderly and, as the heel of her hand caressed his jaw, he tangled lean fingers in her hair and brought her face toward his.

"Sweet. You're so sweet," he whispered between lightly brushing kisses. "My delightful Abby."

"I think you're a delight," she whispered back.

"I *have* missed you."

"I missed you, too," she said, her voice breaking huskily. "So very much, Joel."

His arm went around her waist, muscles tightening as he slipped his hand between her and the mattress. His fingers curved around her, firming his grip, and while slowly drawing her closer he promised, "I'm going to keep you here all night, Abby."

Her eyes met his, saw the steady flame of passion in their dark depths, and felt hypnotized by it. Her arm slipped up over his onto his shoulders. "All night," she repeated breathlessly. "Yes."

"In this bed."

"*Yes.*"

"It's been too long, Abby," he said roughly, his lean powerful body moving against her. "I may never stop making love to you."

"I hope you won't," she confessed. "I don't want you to."

With a rough groan, he gathered her against him. "You mean that?"

Aroused by his provocative promise, her entire body on fire from the touch of his, she nodded. "I mean it."

"You have to now," he warned, turning swiftly to press

her down into the mattress, his long leg heavy as it pinned both hers beneath it.

His dark face filled her vision. To her, he was all that mattered. Nothing else existed then except that boat in the cove, that cabin, that bed, and the two of them.

Abby's arms went around him, pulling him closer still as his mouth claimed her own with rousing insistence. His evocative weight covering her slight frame made her senses swim, made her feel delightfully small and submissive, though she knew that his power over her was actually no greater than hers over him. He had always expected her to participate actively in their loveplay, and she had done so happily. That night was no exception. She brushed her smooth thigh slowly, provocatively, between his, and as his upsurging response accompanying his low groan, muffled by their kiss, conveyed a nearly intolerable need, she found sensuous pleasure in her ability to arouse him.

"Seductress," he huskily called her, even teeth nibbling the tenderness of her parted lips, his tongue tasting their honeyed allure. "You drive me crazy."

Thrill after burning thrill rippled deep inside Abby. "I—want to," she admitted haltingly, "since you drive me crazy, too."

"I've only started," he warned, moving slightly to better explore her lissome body.

She trailed her fingertips along the taut tendons of Joel's neck, then kneaded and massaged the straining muscles of his shoulders and back while his persuasive hands, roaming freely over her silken flesh, conveyed barely restrained passion. Controlling his desire, he stroked the fire of her passion until it blazed with fierce intensity. She pressed close to him, caressed him. Her opening mouth sought his, and as they kissed again and again, longing became a central aching emptiness deep inside her. She couldn't get enough of touching him as he rubbed his palms over the ivory fullness of her breasts, which swelled with the caress.

Playing with the rose-tipped peaks, he teased them to throbbing hard nubs of exquisitely sensitive flesh, then lowered his head and took each one in turn into his mouth.

His fingertips slipped beneath the elastic waist of her panties and pulled down, completely removing them. He blazed a trail of burning kisses across her flat abdomen while slipping his fingers between her thighs. When her legs weakened and moved apart, he moved between them and laid his hands on her thighs, his thumbs brushing upward.

Trembling, Abby opened drowsy bewitching eyes and whispered, "*Love* me, Joel."

"Oh, I'm going to. Not yet, but soon," he promised, then proceeded to make her wild with her need for him. Yet when he later drew one small hand from his shoulder and guided it downward, and she touched him eagerly, his self-control snapped and he lifted her hips to receive him.

Abby's nails pressed down against the contracted muscles of his shoulders, and Joel's filling possession evoked a long tremulous sigh of sheer pleasure. At that moment of union she felt more alive than she had in much too long a time, and the awesome force of her love for him brought tears of joy to her eyes. What had happened that night and what was about to happen was so inalterably right. Predestined.

Joel was still for a moment, cupping her face in his hands, looking down at her, and she was lost in the mesmerizing intensity of his gaze. "Teach me everything," she whispered compulsively, perhaps prompted by a subconscious fear that this might be her final night with him, that this might be her last chance to add to her store of precious memories. The soft light in her aqua eyes beckoned to him. She touched her fingertips to his lips. "Tell me everything I can do to please you."

"And you tell me everything I can do to please you,"

he whispered back, kissing those fingertips as a sudden hot illumination flared in his black eyes. "Start now, Abby."

"Kiss me. Really kiss me again," she complied. And as he did and her lips parted wider, inviting the electrically evocative invasion of his tongue, he began moving once more. She moved with him, meeting his gentle urgings with slowly mounting excitement. The raw, barely leashed power of his lean body, his whispered endearments, and his patient need to give her pleasure all combined to further enhance her love for him. And love heightens passion. As they drifted together to higher and higher plateaus of delight sensations became overpoweringly exquisite, and when Abby was consumed by a driving need to seek completion for herself and Joel, she wound herself around him.

"Now, Joel. *Now*," she murmured, exhilarated when the words in his ear fanned the fires of his passion until it burned out of control. She gasped as he swiftly became less gentle and moved more quickly with more powerful insistence. Suddenly, swiftly, she was borne up to the keenest, most piercing peak of ecstasy. He joined her there, and she softly cried his name as wave after wave of shattering intensity crashed within her, became ripples, then rose to an exquisite crest again before subsiding to the warmest, deepest level of fulfillment.

Joel's breathing was as ragged as her own as they lay together in the sweet aftermath, limbs entangled, sheets crumpled beneath them, and Abby's perfume mingling with Joel's after-shave on both their bodies. Together their heartbeats began to slow, and utterly content, Abby buried her cheek in the hollow of Joel's shoulder before stretching up lazily as a kitten to seek his lips with her own.

They exchanged languid satisfied kisses, held each other, looked at each other, enjoyed each other, until Abby's thickly lashed eyelids began to flutter shut. Almost immediately she became aware that Joel's hands were moving over her again, conveying a certain demand, and her eyes opened, widened, as she gazed at the lean sun-bronzed face she loved so much.

"You made me wait for you too long," he told her, moving to encircle her breasts in a series of burning kisses. The radiant heat of his body seared her creamy skin. He pressed the edge of a forefinger against her chin, tugged at it gently to part her lips, and kissed her, his hard mouth taking hers with swiftly graduating demand. Several moments later he lifted his head and smiled down at her. "Much too long, so we won't be going to sleep just yet."

With a secretive little smile directed at Joel, Abby put her arms around his neck. The firm, full roundness of her breasts grazed his chest, then yielded, womanly soft to more inflexible muscular male flesh, as Joel crushed her against him. When rising desire turned Abby's nipples into hard nubbles that rubbed his skin, Joel's passionate whisper was muffled in the tousled thickness of her hair. Then his hard lips were plundering her mouth again, and within seconds sleep was the last thing she wanted.

Their lovemaking was more playful, less feverish, than before, yet no less fulfilling. They explored each other, delighted in each other, *knew* each other in such perfect intimacy that when completion came, they were swept up in a whirlwind of physical and emotional rapture, drifting down together from the summit again. Lying in the circle of Joel's arms afterward, indolent and deliciously relaxed, Abby curled closely against him. The fact that Joel's slow, steady breathing soon indicated he was no longer awake scarcely registered in her brain before she too slipped into a sleep more peaceful than she had experienced in weeks.

Abby awoke after seven the next morning. The gentle rocking motion of the sloop nearly lulled her back to sleep again, but at last she roused herself sufficiently to pry her eyelids open. Contentment enveloped her, and the remembrance of the previous night caused her heart to skip several beats. Tilting her head back, she looked up at Joel's face and was momentarily breathless from the magnitude of her love for him. With a slow smile, she lightly touched the dark stubble of a night's growth of beard on his chin, then pressed her lips gently as a butterfly's wing against his brown skin where it hardened over his collarbone. Taking care not to disturb him, she raised his muscular arm flung across her waist and moved from beneath it to slip out of bed.

She opened the door next to the private companionway and entered what she called the adjoining bathroom but what seasoned sailors called the head. She splashed water on her face, patted it dry with a fluffy towel, then, lacking a toothbrush, applied toothpaste to the tip of her forefinger and cleaned her teeth the best she could. Choosing the smaller of two terry cloth robes hanging on the back of the door, she slipped into it and, a few minutes later, tiptoed across the stateroom to the door that opened into the main cabin.

In the forward galley she found instant coffee and cups, then set a pan of water on a burner of the gas stove to heat. Through the porthole above the sink she saw the early morning sun glimmering on the water and gazed out, allowing her thoughts, as they so often did, to wander to Joel. She wrapped her arms across her breasts, hugging the memory of the night before close to her. She felt no regrets. She had needed Joel so much, and he had wanted her. And because he had taken precautions, he had eliminated the fear of pregnancy. It did hurt a bit to know that he had come aboard the *Sea Nymph* prepared for a night of intimacy. How sure he must have been that she would at last allow this to become a "sex holiday." A casual romp for him. Yet his taking of proper precautions had made it possible for her to surrender to her need for him and to his desires. And, that morning, she could only be glad she had.

Lost in thought, Abby wasn't aware that Joel was out of bed and had left the stateroom until he actually entered the galley. Magnificently virile and dark-skinned in the other white terry robe she had seen in the bathroom, he leaned against the teak bar that separated the galley from the main cabin and rubbed a hand over his dark hair.

"You're boiling," he announced, casually lifting one finger toward the pan on the stove in which the water was bubbling merrily.

Abby dragged her gaze from him and laughed at herself while removing the pan from the burner. "Well, I hope you like *very* hot coffee. I must have been daydreaming. I didn't even notice the water had begun to simmer. While we're waiting for it to cool a little, I found an unopened box of cookies in the cabinet . . . if you're hungry. I'm afraid that's about all I can offer; there aren't any eggs."

Shaking his head, Joel settled himself at the small table, extending his long legs out before him. "Coffee's all I want, anyway. Black, please."

Abby nodded. While she padded around the galley, measuring freeze-dried granules into both mugs, then finding sugar for her own coffee, she sensed he was watching her every move. It rather pleased her that he was, and she met his dark gaze directly when she carried both mugs to the table and sat down across from him.

In comfortable silence they both took cautious sips of the steaming coffee, and Abby was unable to prevent herself from watching Joel, too. Before joining her in the galley he had shaved, and she thought about how smooth his carved tan face would be if she touched it. She was enjoying sharing the morning with him, isolated from the rest of the world on the boat.

But perhaps she was enjoying everything too much. Suddenly that frightening, insidious thought took root in her mind, and when Joel took one of her small hands in both of his, confusion swept over her.

"It's still early, Abby," he said softly, coaxingly. "Come back to bed."

With the words, her heart seemed to plummet. Fears she had been able to suppress the night before rose unbidden to haunt her. Although she still didn't regret what she had already allowed to happen, something deep within her was warning her not to allow it to happen again. She loved Joel too much for her own good, and she could see herself becoming more and more involved with him again. Losing Joel a second time would be even more painful than it had been the first time, and Abby cringed inwardly at the debilitating prospect. Difficult as it was going to be to refuse Joel now, she must. She *must*.

Eyes downcast, staring at the tabletop, she tried to withdraw her hand from his and was appalled by the sharp stab of pain that ripped through her chest when he wouldn't release her. She shook her head. "Going back to bed isn't a good idea, is it? I mean, Faye must be very worried about us, and if we don't get back to Fairfields soon, she might have the law out beating the bushes for us."

"Of course she won't. She must know we're together, and that's precisely what she's been wanting," Joel countered, rising, smiling indulgently when he tried to draw her up beside him and she held back. His thumb brushed caressingly over the backs of her fingers. "Abby, love, Faye really isn't worried, so come back to bed with me."

Terrified she might succumb to his seductive tone, the arousing touch, and knowing she must *not,* Abby forcibly removed her hand from his. "I don't want to go back to bed," she lied, making herself look up at him. "Last night . . . last night just happened. I'm not sure how. Maybe I was just caught up in the magic of the ball, maybe even bewitched by the dress I was wearing. Anyway, I wasn't thinking straight then, but I am now."

Joel's curse was explicit. Anger glinted like glowing coals in his eyes. Towering over her, feet wide apart, he muttered through clenched teeth, "That damn dress had nothing to do with anything. You wanted me last night as much as I wanted you. You still do."

"No, I—"

"No more damn games, Abby," he cautioned, and in one fluid motion he hauled her up from the chair and swept her off her feet up into his arms, which tightened like bands of steel around her when she struggled. Joel smiled rather wickedly when Abby realized resistence was futile and lay still. He strode from the galley across the main cabin into the stateroom. "What you started last night, you're going to finish. We're going to spend the rest of this vacation *together,* really together, like we were last night. No strings attached—just the way you want it and the way I want it, too. Understand, Abby? I won't tolerate your teasing any longer. You went too far last night. Now you can't go back."

Dropped with little gentleness onto the mattress and pillow, Abby gasped, blue eyes widening as she looked up at him. This was a Joel she had never before seen. Determination was like a driving force in him, and even the inflexible line of his body conveyed relentlessness. He had never looked as big and powerful and virile to her as he did right then, and she was overwhelmingly aware of a male strength she was physically powerless against. Yet, she knew another way to handle him. When she moved swiftly and tried to swing off the far side of the bed but was stopped by Joel's arm coming around her waist to toss her back down onto the mattress again, she laughed up at him and fought her own rising excitement.

"Caveman tactics don't suit you," she told him, only a concerted effort keeping a note of odd exhilaration out of her voice. "Let me go. You don't want an unwilling partner in bed."

"Oh, but you won't be unwilling for long," he whispered, bending over her with a provocative smile. "And we both know that."

She shook her head, refusing to give in to him, despite the fact that the encounter seemed to be transforming into a game—a game she rather enjoyed playing, though she knew she should not. She stared coolly at him. "You can't make me respond."

"I won't have to. You'll want to respond the way you responded last night. You're a tremendously passionate young woman, Abby. Now, stop fighting the inevitable and relax. You're going to enjoy every minute of this," he promised. And, smiling, he dropped a hand down to the belt of her robe.

CHAPTER SIX

Joel untied Abby's belt and tossed the ends aside. Although that small action made her heart race, she lay tense and unyielding, feigning supreme indifference. Determined not to surrender self-control and respond with passion as he expected, she merely stared at him through the thick fringe of her long lashes, waiting for him to open the robe, steeling herself to show no visible reaction when he did.

As if he had read her mind and decided to deliberately catch her off guard, Joel left the robe around her and instead only traced his fingertips along the curve of her neck, then lowered his head to brush his firm lips across the pulse throbbing in her throat.

Unprepared for such a tender caress, Abby involuntarily arched her neck in an attempt to escape it, and when Joel laughed knowingly, she cursed herself for her reaction. Certain Joel would quickly become bored if she just lay there, immobile and totally unresponsive, she managed to achieve that objective for several seconds until he slowly pushed the robe off one shoulder. His mouth sought her skin, tantalizing her nerve endings with tiny nibbling kisses, sending a thrill up and down Abby's spine. Catching her lower lip between her teeth, she fought against the weakness slowly invading her limbs and the warmth suffusing her traitorous body. It was an uphill battle, however, and when Joel suddenly bestowed a feathery kiss on the curve of her breast, she could lie still no longer.

"Don't," she demanded as icily as she could, catching his face between her hands. "I don't want—"

"Hush, I know what you want," he murmured, his warm lips covering hers to halt the continuation of her attempted protest. He played with her mouth, teased it, tasted the sweetness within, and while one arm encircled her waist, his other hand stroked her hair.

Successive waves of warmth were washing over Abby now, each one in its turn burning more deeply and making her weaker. When her fingers, on his cheeks, began to ache with her growing need to return his caresses, she removed them, intending to let her hands fall to her sides again, but seemingly of their own volition, they dropped onto Joel's shoulders instead. She groaned inwardly, distraught at how easy she was making this for him. Common sense was screaming at her to resist him, but the warnings gradually became so faint, she could no longer even hear them. Love was not to be so easily dismissed. It never is. And Abby's love for Joel was strong and true. Four months earlier it had compelled her to leave him for his sake, and now, as it had last night, it was surging up in her again, becoming a vital force she could not contain. Her hands curved over his shoulders, gripping lightly, and she found herself allowing her lips, which had been pressed tightly together, to be coaxed apart slowly. Part of her wanted to surrender unequivocally, but uncertainty held her back, making her unwilling, actually unable, to give as freely as she had given the night before.

If Joel had been encouraged by her slight yielding and

rushed her, he would have undoubtedly succeeded only in strengthening her self-protective need to resist him. He didn't rush, however. He moved to lie on his side next to her, turned her to him, and, with incredible finesse, took her small chin between his thumb and forefinger, tilting her face this way and that while he kissed the delicate arches of her brows, closed eyelids, and the slight hollows beneath the contours of her high cheekbones. Abby's breath mingled with Joel's when his lips touched hers for too brief an instant, then slipped away to feather over her satiny skin.

Despite the fact that the gentle seduction was becoming increasingly effective, Abby was still startled when Joel slid one hand inside the untied robe. Her eyes flew open and met the unfathomable darkness of his as his fingertips grazed across her bare midriff, over her side, and around to the small of her back. Appalled by the sensations aroused by his touch, she tensed and tried to pull away from him.

"Be still," he commanded roughly, determination hardening his jaw again as his hand clamped relentlessly over her hipbone to hold her fast. Hard brown eyes impaled the softness of her own, yet his tone gentled considerably when he repeated, "Abby, be still."

She was still, deliberately so, until his sensitive roving fingertips began climbing her spine in slow circular motions to probe every inch of her delicate bone structure and baby-smooth skin. An uncontrollable tremor ran through Abby's slight frame and her body weakened and relaxed. She heard Joel's muted murmur of satisfaction and felt a desperate need to resist him yet couldn't. Then she could only feel, could only find delight in, the firm pressure exerted by the heel of his hand as he massaged her shoulders. Then the backs of his fingers were descending her spine, following the curving bend of the small of her back and rising over the gentle swell of her hips. When his hand at last came to rest on her firmly rounded buttocks and squeezed gently, Abby had to bite back the soft moan that rose in her throat.

Involuntarily she reached toward him, but his hand came from beneath the robe to catch hers before it touched him, and suddenly he was removing her arm from its sleeve.

"Joel, *don't,*" she protested weakly as he pushed the robe back. Practically naked, only her other arm still covered by the robe, Abby felt his warm breath feather caressingly over her bare skin. "No! No, no."

"Oh, yes, Abby, yes," he whispered, unmoved by her pleas, his hand gripping her trim waist to pull her a few inches nearer. "Don't talk now. Kiss me."

Incredibly she obeyed, but even as she rubbed her parted lips across the sensuous lines of his, she was trying to catch his hand to prevent him from touching her more intimately. She failed. Instead, he caught her wrist and swiftly turned her over onto her stomach, pinning one arm beneath her while raising the other up beside her head. Afraid of what he might do to her next and even more afraid of how she might react to whatever he did, Abby squeezed her eyes shut. She felt the heavy hand resting in the center of her back being replaced by his other one, and with her face to one side on the pillow, she peered out from beneath the feathery fringe of her lashes. Her heart seemed to leap up in her throat and palpitate wildly there. Joel was naked now, kneeling beside her, and the sight of him made her senses reel. She couldn't stop looking at him, spellbound by his broad chest, tapered waist, lean hips, and strongly formed thighs. She had never felt more vulnerable than she did in that moment when he bent down over her. An explosive tremor fluttered up from deep inside her to run visibly over her as he scattered aggressive nipping kisses over the entire surface of her back. He swept an exploring hand over the rise of her hips, along the backs

95

of her thighs and calves, and even down to the sensitized soles of her feet.

Abby trembled weakly, and, realizing how effective his caresses had been, Joel spanned her waist with capable hands, turned her over onto her back again, and moved her legs apart to kneel between them. His piercing gaze captured and held hers as he removed her robe completely, then lifted her up a bit to pull it from beneath her.

"God, you're beautiful—so very beautiful, Abby," he said unevenly, his narrowed eyes playing over the swift rise and fall of her breasts. "I never want to stop touching you." And as if to prove his words, his hands glided upward from her waist to take possession of her breasts, cupping and squeezing gently the mounds of flesh. Joel lowered his head, and his mouth covered hers, parting her lips with near-savage demand and conveying an insatiable hunger that made her heart pound in her ears. She made a soft sound, a sound of defeat and surrender and delight, as she was suddenly kissing him back. His lips hardened on her own and exerted a slight twisting pressure that brought her upward into his muscular arms, which molded her supple young body to his.

Abby felt faint with the sensual pleasure that rushed hotly through her, and with her softness crushed against the unyielding plane of his chest, she wanted him never to release her and protested softly when he lowered her back onto the mattress again. But then his hands were playing over her breasts once more, like licking flames over her skin, arousing her rose-tipped peaks. A quickening shaft of pleasure made Abby dizzy with longing and she arched against him, seeking fulfillment and finding intense pleasure in the lithe smooth body that lightly pressed hers down. His hot bare flesh enthralled her, and she wound her arms around his waist and traced the corded muscles of his back with eager fingertips.

When Joel raised himself slightly once more, Abby tilt-

96

ed her head back, exposing the graceful line of her neck to his lips, which grazed down to the frantic pulse in her throat and the scented hollow just beneath, then lowered to the shadowed valley between her breasts. He took them in his hands yet again, as if he were compelled to caress such warmly resilient womanly flesh, and with his touch they surged full and taut against his fingers. Her involuntary physical response seemed an invitation, one he did not refuse. Placing a hand around her waist, entangling the other in the glorious thickness of her hair, he leaned down to kiss one throbbing tumescent nipple, then its twin, before his tongue began to flick lovingly over and around each firm pink tip.

Stiletto-sharp sensations plunged through Abby and she was lost. Her hands moved feverishly back and forth across Joel's shoulders. She slowly turned her head from side to side on the pillow as his lips and tongue and gently nibbling teeth continued to possess the desire-swollen roseate peaks of her breasts. He was making her wild. *"Joel!"* she breathed softly, taking his face between her hands and urging his mouth to hers. His lips descended, taking hers with heady demand, and as his weight settled a bit more heavily on her, her supple slender body seemed to melt into his. Acquiescent and pliant now, she entangled her long shapely legs with his. But as she felt his surging passion rigid against her bare abdomen, his large hand curved over her delicate hipbone and pressed her down against the bed, denying her contact with his aroused masculinity.

Abby produced a low, almost beseeching sound. Her eyes flickered open to see the slight victorious smile that moved Joel's finely chiseled mouth before it came down to claim hers again. With coaxing aggression, his marauding lips devoured hers, his warm minty breath filling her throat. She shivered as the tip of his tongue rubbed over the tender veined flesh of her inner cheek and tasted the inside of her mouth. Abby's lips parted and closed, parted and closed, on the lower curve of his as she moved her slender arms and searching hands over the broad expanse of his back. She pressed closer to him, yet his hands on her hips still held her at some distance, still denied her the more intimate contact she longed for.

The feel of rippling muscles beneath her palms made her ache for him, yet his hands rose to her shoulders and held her down while he raised up to kneel above her once again. Her breathing quickened as he branded her flat abdomen with a zigzag of scorching kisses, then rubbed his lips along her upper thigh, his teeth gently nibbling tender, highly sensitive flesh. Joel's knee slipped between her legs and parted them, and the empty aching within Abby intensified to an almost intolerable level. She was alive with the passion only he could assuage, yet he still didn't take what she was so obviously ready to give. Instead, he stroked her arms and legs, feathered his fingertips over her breasts, and touched her lips with teasing kisses.

Running her fingers through his thick hair, Abby lay watching him, eyes dark blue with yearning. Now she knew he was making her wait for him, and when he lay down on his side next to her, she realized he intended to make her wait longer still. She suppressed a smile. Although the intensity of her desire was making her light-headed, she still had the presence of mind to know intuitively that she could turn the tables on him and, turning over to face him, she began.

Smiling at him drowsily, she drew a provocatively light hand along his side, over the lean line of his hip to his muscular thigh, then lazily drew it back up again, fluttering across his shoulder to curve it around the back of his neck. She pulled herself closer to him, close enough to rain little kisses over his lean cheeks, often allowing them to brush the very corners of his mouth. But when he murmured an incomprehensible word and cupped her jaw in one hand to try to bring her lips to his, she didn't let him. She lowered her head instead, seeking the smooth brown skin stretched taut across his collarbone. She planted tiny breeze-light kisses there and up the rising column of his neck while the heel of her hand stroking his chest found the hard nubble of a flat nipple in a bed of fine dark hair. She rubbed the tip of one finger around and over the nub until Joel's breathing quickened. She was content . . . but not finished. She had become the aggressor and was enjoying every minute. With a boldness she had never thought herself capable of, she took one of his hands and brought it to her breast, pressing it down against her warm flesh. Pleased when his long fingers probed the rounded slopes, she proceeded with her mission.

Brushing back the dark swath of hair that had fallen across Joel's forehead, Abby moved nearer still, her parted lips following the strong line of his jaw to his ear. With the tip of her tongue she traced small circles in the hollow beneath it, then took the fleshy lobe between her teeth and nibbled, her senses swirling when his hand on her breast tightened. Whispering words she had never imagined she would say, she gently raked her fingernails over Joel's back, then brought a more caressing hand around and across the flat hardness of his abdomen, sending a shudder through him.

"*Temptress,*" he groaned, his mouth taking hers with devastating force. "Shameless vixen."

"Tormentor," she called him, then caught her breath in a gasp as he suddenly rolled onto his back and brought her over on top of him. His eyes, glinting with passion, bored into hers. Watching her face, he pressed her hips down, forcibly lifting his own, and entered her. Her soft cry of pleasure mingled with the deeper, rougher tone of his. And as he possessed her completely and a tremulous smile touched her lips, his answering smile conveyed intimate understanding.

Cupping the back of her neck in one hand, he brought her face down until his lips were taking the soft shape of hers, hungrily savoring their sweetness as she settled with warm fluidity onto him. His arms came tight around her, imprisoning her slight form against the hard, yet lithe, length of his body, and he released her mouth only to whisper into her ear, "What a captivating little wench you are, Abby."

"And I could call you an incurable seducer of young women," she retorted, laughing down at him until the fiery gleam in his eyes and the muscle ticking in his hardening jaw took her breath away. She gazed wonderingly at his tan face and was inundated with abiding love for him, a love she could no longer give in words, perhaps, but had to give to him somehow. Her own desires aroused again to a fever pitch simply by the way he was looking at her, Abby raised up slightly and began to move with an inviting sensual grace born of an age-old feminine instinct. The obvious certainty that she was giving Joel pleasure made her happy, and she smiled as his hands roamed urgently over her, touching her face, cupping her ivory breasts, spanning her waist.

Abby ran her fingertips across Joel's chest, feeling his muscles ripple and contract beneath her light touch. Her palms glided over his strong upper arms, and as they did he gripped her elbows and he pulled her down toward him.

"Abby, come here," he muttered hoarsely, managing with great effort to exercise strict control over needs she was already very close to fulfilling. As she leaned over him, her golden hair tumbling forward like a silk curtain around her face, the peaks of her breasts brushing his chest, he kissed her shoulders and the hollow at the base of her throat.

He had become the aggressor once more, his hands, on her hips, guiding them in slow circular motions as he waited for the response that came quickly. Abby's breathing quickened audibly with the increasing sensations racing through her. Her lips found Joel's and she gloried in the compelling demand of his kiss. She pressed against him, allowing him to bear most of her weight as the long leisurely strokes of his hard body corresponded perfectly with the slow movements of her own. She felt Joel's breath stir a tendril of her hair. Love for him overflowed in her, as pure and constant as water flowing from a mountain spring, and as his hand traveled across the small of her back, the caress honed the sensations he was creating in her to a sharp edge. Astoundingly soon, Abby was irrevocably caught up in a maelstrom of delight. She clung to Joel, her lips parting eagerly to the firmness of his, and some unslowing momentum was spinning her upward . . . upward toward . . .

Joel suddenly ceased moving and held her still, whispering softly, "Not yet, love, not yet." His arms wrapped securely around her as she relaxed against him, her breath coming in soft swift little gasps. She burrowed her hot face in his neck and, as anticipation mounted in her, burning like a raging fire over her body, she drew her hands down along his lean sides and murmured his name, making a soft pleasurable sound as he began moving again.

They made love slowly, lazily. With unrushed deliberation, Joel once more swept Abby up near the pinnacle of ecstasy, then was still, further heightening her passion and subsequently her delight when he at last took her beyond all rational thought. Exquisite pleasure washed through her in hot rippling waves and she clung to him, kissing him with ardent abandon.

"*Abby,*" he murmured roughly.

She felt almost faint with excitement when he swiftly turned over and brought her beneath him, hard pillaging lips claiming hers while he took his own satisfaction with an urgent demand that made her feel infinitely desired.

Some moments later they lay in each other's arms, Abby cuddling close to Joel's side as he tenderly stroked her tousled hair. As she sighed contentedly she noticed that the midmorning sun was spilling bright light down the open companionway into the stateroom. She smiled, leaned her head back a bit, and shared her smile with him.

"It must be at least ten o'clock, judging by how high the sun is in the sky," she told him. "I didn't realize it was that late."

Joel shrugged carelessly, grinning. "You know the old saying: 'Time flies when you're having fun.' "

Abby gently nudged his ribs with an elbow but returned his grin. "Joke if you like, but I hope you know this means everyone will be up and about at Fairfields when we get back. And since we'll be dressed in our ball finery, it'll be pretty obvious that we spent the night together somewhere."

"It'll be obvious, all right," he replied wryly. "I'm just wondering whether Faye will welcome us back with a standing ovation or a trumpet salute. Surely she'll want to mark the occasion somehow as a milestone in her matchmaking career."

Abby laughed. "She *has* been very blatant about trying to throw us together since we got to Fairfields, but she means well. We're her friends; she cares about us."

"Yes. That's exactly why she worries about you, why it bothers her very much that there seems to be a part of you that you never share with other people, something you seem to need to keep deep inside. That bothers me too, Abby," Joel said, his tone very serious. Lifting her chin with one finger, he made her look at him and his eyes intently scanned her uptilted face as if he hoped to find answers to his questions there. He shook his head. "And I have to admit I'm as confused as hell. I know there's

102

always a definite reserve about you *except* when I take you to bed. Then you hold nothing back, and I wonder how there could be anything in your life you couldn't share with me. But there is something, Abby. There must be, or you'd have no reason to act the way you did in the galley this morning."

When he paused expectantly, watching her as if awaiting an explanation, Abby hastily lowered her eyes, unable to continue looking directly at him. Her mind groped for some reasonable excuse for admittedly erratic behavior, but in the end she came up with nothing better than the same old lie. "You're trying to make a mystery woman of me again," she chided, trying to dismiss his too perceptive remarks with light laughter. "I can only tell you one more time that you're mistaken about me. I'm not trying to hide anything from anybody. As for this morning, I had decided that we should get right back to Fairfields so Faye wouldn't worry about us. That's really all there was to it." She looked back up to gauge Joel's reaction to her words, then moaned inwardly. Everything in his somber expression hinted that he didn't believe her, and she repeated more emphatically, "Really."

"Prove it, then," he demanded, the strange light in his dark eyes reinforcing the challenge in his words. Sitting up in the bed, he brought her up onto her knees beside him, his hands gripping her shoulders lightly. "No more games like this morning's. No more sudden turnarounds in the way you act toward me. All right, Abby?"

Entrapped by her own lies, she could only nod agreeably. "All right," she promised. But was it a promise she could keep? Obviously she would have to try, if only in an attempt to allay his suspicion that she was hiding something from him. She suppressed a sigh and conceded. "I know I act rather moody sometimes, and that's irritating. I'll try to change."

"And we will be spending the rest of this vacation

together, right, Abby?" he persisted, his fingers fleetingly pressing into her shoulders. "Really together, like we were last night and have been this morning."

"All right," she responded automatically, suddenly feeling as if she were being pulled along toward a fate beyond her control. Before she could try to hide it, the one real truth in her life tumbled out. "It is what I want, Joel. I want us to be together."

A smile that seemed almost triumphant quickly touched his hard mouth, then was gone in an instant. His hands lightened on her and he leaned forward to kiss the tip of her small nose. "Well, since that's finally settled, I guess we'd better start thinking about getting back to Fairfields. I'm starved. How about you?"

"I'm hungry, too."

"Good." Taking her hand in his, he rose from the bed with powerful grace and stood over her. "Come on, then. We'll shower, dress, then sail back."

Noticing the rather wicked gleam in his eyes, Abby had to laugh and, mercifully, the laughter eased her tension. She shook her head in mock admonition. "Joel, you know very well that if we shower together, we'll end up right back in this bed and very probably starve to death before we can get back to Fairfields."

Joel raised his dark brows, his expression exaggerated with surprise. "Are you really insinuating you can't trust me to keep my hands off you?"

"I'm not insinuating anything," she retorted perkily. "I'm saying outright that I can't trust you."

"Incredible," he murmured, amusement edging his deep voice as, with a sharp tug of her hands, he brought her out of the bed. "How dare you doubt the trustworthiness of a revered physician like me?"

As Abby allowed him to lead her into the diminutive bathroom she was happy, as she almost always was when she was with Joel. He was good for her. He made her feel alive, and although her promise to spend the vacation with him had seemed crazy and potentially harmful, she decided then that it was a promise she wanted to keep. After all, she would be risking hurt only for herself. "No strings attached," Joel had said, which meant he no longer expected or *wanted* anything more from her than a temporary intimate involvement. Abby had always been a cautious person with an eye on the future, but that moment seemed the right time to change. Until Joel lost interest in her, she would stay with him, grabbing as much happiness as she could for as long as she could, and repeatedly telling herself that she wouldn't live to regret her brief fling at living only for the present.

CHAPTER SEVEN

"Catch it! Catch it!" Faye yelled excitedly, urging David on as he ran across the beach, arms uplifted in his quest to catch the softball descending in its arc. Unfortunately, he stumbled across a piece of driftwood partially embedded in the sand and fell sprawling but unhurt in a clump of sea oats. About thirty feet beyond him the ball landed with a plop in wet sand, then rolled slowly into the surf. Faye heaved a thoroughly disgruntled sigh, then shouted, "Well, for heaven's sake, David, you should have caught *that* one."

"Huh! That's easy for you to say. You didn't even try to catch it, and if you wouldn't keep pitching Abby balls so easy to hit, I wouldn't be running my legs off," David shouted back, picking himself up, dusting himself off, and scowling at the grains of sand that clung tenaciously to his khaki shorts and bare thighs. Walking back toward his wife, he grumbled aloud, "Abby hits a home run every time she bats. Knocks every ball you throw her from here to eternity, so don't blame me for not catching something a pro baseball player couldn't catch. I run after them as hard as I can."

"Hah! You call that running?" Faye countered, the teasing note evident in her voice, although she tried to sound disgusted. "I've seen ducks waddle faster than that."

"I haven't seen you breaking any track records either," her husband retorted, a smile twitching at his lips. "Besides, I'm too big to run fast in sand. Sink into it up to my ankles."

"Excuses, excuses. Why don't you just admit that . . ."

Completing her leisurely jog around the bases, Abby rounded toward home and exchanged an amused grin with Joel, who stood at home base, leaning nonchalantly, with one hand, on the bat. As she reached him, adding another run to their score, he slipped an arm over her shoulders and briefly hugged her against his side.

"Way to go, slugger," he teased, then lowered his voice to add, "How *did* you learn to hit a ball like that?"

"Spent most of my childhood summers playing softball with neighborhood kids," she explained. Tucking a wayward strand of sun-washed hair behind one ear, she inclined her head toward Faye and David, who were still "discussing" their respective athletic abilities. "Look at them, at it again. They do love teasing each other, don't they?"

"They certainly have their playful bickering routine down pat," Joel agreed with a knowing smile. "Personally, I think they have these little 'spats' just for the chance to make up afterward, which, come to think of it, isn't a bad idea." Appraising Abby's shapely figure with an exaggerated provocative grin, he went into his amazingly convincing impression of Clark Gable as Rhett Butler. "My dear, would you care to engage in a very friendly spat?"

"Later, perhaps," she replied, coquettishly looking up at him out of the corners of her eyes. "We're not alone now, and I do believe we'd need privacy to make up properly."

Their muted laughter didn't go unnoticed, and within seconds Faye and David joined them at home base. David, still pretending to glower irritably at his wife, lifted his huge shoulders, then allowed them to drop in a theatrically dejected shrug.

"I guess we might as well concede defeat," he announced with an over dramatic sigh. "You two are too many runs up on us; we can never catch up now."

"Don't feel too bad, Dave," Joel consoled, amusement gleaming in his eyes. "Abby just told me she had plenty of practice playing softball when she was a little girl."

"Practically a pro, huh? No wonder we lost. Not quite fair, Joel, for you to have a semipro as a teammate, while I have Faye," David said, barely able to suppress a grin as he tugged a strand of his wife's auburn hair. "Maybe if you'd practice a lot, honey, you could hit the ball as hard as Abby does. Maybe you could just *hit* it once in a while."

"Basketball's my game," Faye replied archly, turning her nose up at him. "Too bad you don't have one at all, sport."

Unable to think of anything to top that cutting remark, David roared with laughter. A bear of a man, he lifted his wife off her feet and planted a kiss squarely on her lips, ending their pseudoargument as quickly as it had begun. After lowering her to the ground again, he left his arm draped across her shoulders as he grinned at Abby and Joel. "Oh, well, she's a pretty good wife, even if she can't hit, catch, or pitch a softball. Anyway, I can't blame her entirely for our losing; next time we'll know better than to play against a seasoned veteran like Abby." He smiled at his houseguests, a special, reassuring message in his eyes for Abby. "What a combination—beauty, brains, and athletic ability all in one fantastic package. If I wasn't already a happily married man . . ."

"You won't be for long if you don't stop flirting with my friends right in front of my eyes," Faye warned, but smiled as she took him by the arm. "Let's go back to the house, honey. The sun's getting too hot for me; I want a shower and a cool drink."

After Abby and Joel expressed their desire to remain on the beach to go for a swim, the married couple left them, walking arm in arm past the bungalow to where they had parked their car. When the sound of their engine faded and the beach was quiet except for the swish of the surf and the calling of swooping gulls, Joel turned Abby to face him. Slowly he began to undo the buttons of her sleeveless blouse, beneath which she wore a swimsuit.

After Abby had allowed him to remove both blouse and shorts, she watched as he stripped off his own shorts and navy polo shirt, down to the white swimming trunks. Smiling slightly to herself, she doubted she could ever get enough simply of looking at him, and when he glanced over at her and gave her one of his slow, easy smiles in return for hers, joy filled her. For three entire days in a row since the fateful decision she had made in the cabin on the *Sea Nymph,* she had felt truly happy. Living for the moment had an almost addictive appeal, and she never allowed herself to remember that eventually the future becomes the present. She had no desire to look ahead and refused to do so. All that mattered was the here and now, because that was all she dared let matter.

Without any of the hesitation that might have accompanied the gesture only days earlier, she slipped her hand into Joel's when they had laid their folded clothing on the railing surrounding the outdoor shower. Her fingers entwined with his as they walked onto the beach to the towel they had spread out earlier. Dropping down onto her knees, Abby took a long deep breath of brine-scented air.

"Umm, it's nice to have the beach to ourselves," she said softly, then qualified her statement. "Of course, I'm glad Faye and David joined us for a while; they're always fun to be around."

His gaze on her, his expression oddly watchful, Joel came down on the towel beside Abby. "They have a terrific relationship, don't you think?" he asked rhetorically. "They're always so open and honest with each other; that's the main reason they're such a perfect couple."

Nearly wincing at the sudden little catch in her chest, Abby looked away from him, scooped up sand in one hand, and watched it trickle between her fingers to form a tiny mound. "Faye's such an extrovert," she declared expressionlessly after a second. "She's open and honest with everyone."

"That's true to a certain extent," Joel conceded, his tone low, serious. "But I'm sure David knows her in ways no one else can. I doubt there's anything she wouldn't tell him. There aren't any secrets between them."

"Oh, surely there must be a few," Abby murmured, uneasiness becoming dread because she knew only too well exactly where this conversation was leading. "David is a doctor, after all, and it would be very improper for him to tell Faye everything. I'm sure there are many secrets about his patients he keeps exclusively to himself."

"Damn it, Abby, don't try to evade the real issue," Joel said sharply, his heavy hand on her shoulder half turning her around to him. "You know damn well I'm not talking about doctor-patient confidences. That's professional, and I'm talking about Faye's and David's deepest personal thoughts and feelings. That's what they share completely."

"Just what is it you're getting at?" Abby asked, though she knew. "I get the distinct impression you're leading up to something."

"How astute of you. Of course I'm leading up to something. I'm asking you again to tell me what it is that's bothering you."

Abby threw up her hands in feigned exasperation. "Good heavens, Joel, are you starting this again? I thought I'd finally managed to convince you that you'd simply been misled by Faye's overactive imagination. Nothing whatsoever is bothering me, and I thought you realized that."

"I almost believed you when you told me that the other day on the boat, but now I can't," he said, his tone gentling as he brushed the back of his hand across her cheek. "During the past three days we've been closer than ever before, and more than once I've seen a sudden darkness come into your eyes, and then you're always very still for a second or two. It's something I don't think you're even aware of, but I am and—"

"You're trying to take me apart again to see what makes me tick, but you're really wasting your time," she answered, her smile concealing the urgent need she felt to convince him. "You already do know everything there is to know about me. Considering our relationship, how could you not?"

"Intimacy with a woman doesn't tell a man everything about her," Joel murmured, leaning over to kiss her with incredible gentleness, his lips brushing hers slowly, coaxingly. "If there is something bothering you, tell me, please. Surely you know you can tell me anything."

Yes, anything *except* the truth about her genetic heritage. Even as she thought that, she could still feel her will bending to the persuasive tenderness of his kiss and to the sheer vital force of his personality. For a fleeting instant she wished she *could* tell him the truth, but some pride and much fear of his reaction should she even utter the word *hemophilia* assured her silence once again. Since theirs was now a "no-strings-attached" relationship, her silence couldn't eventually hurt him but *could* save her considerable pain right then. Three successive days of happiness had intensified her very natural need to experience more

111

like them. She didn't dare risk letting the truth bring such a precious time to an unnecessarily premature end, no matter how persuasive Joel's kisses were or how forceful his personality.

With great effort she willed herself to resist his whispered endearments and cajoling reminders that she could tell him anything and was able to return his kiss, then slowly bring an end to it without betraying any anxiety that would heighten his suspicions. She hopped to her feet, gave Joel the easiest, most unperturbed smile she could muster, and reached down for his hands.

"If anything was bothering me, I'd tell you, I promise. Okay?" she said lightly, and was relieved to see something akin to uncertainty flit over his carved features before vanishing again. She pulled at his hands, urging him up beside her. "But since nothing except the heat is bothering me right now, let's swim. Race you to the water."

As she ran with long-legged grace into the frothing surf, it occurred to her that she was becoming fairly proficient at living only from moment to moment. It was an ability alien to her true nature, however, and since it could very well be short-lived, she decided she'd be wise to make the most of it then.

Immediately after lunch the next day, Abby and Joel walked through the main hall toward the front door, each carrying a tennis racket and a can of balls. Feeling particularly lighthearted, Abby impulsively executed a perfect pirouette in front of the oval gilt-framed mirror to her left, simply to observe the swirling of her tennis skirt around her legs.

"Bravo," Joel murmured, eyeing her appreciatively. When she responded with a demure curtsy, they laughed softly together and continued toward the door.

"Oh, I'm glad I heard you going out." Faye hailed them, hurrying out of the living room. She grimaced apologetically. "I have to ask a favor of you, Abby. You know I persuaded my niece, Valerie, to let me keep little Robert today, because the poor girl's hardly had a minute to herself since he was born. She really needed a break. Well, anyway, Mama just called me, saying her lumbago's flared up and hurts too much for her to drive herself to the doctor. I'm going to take her and I was hoping you wouldn't mind too much watching Robert for an hour or so, two at the most. He's just been fed and is sleeping. Shouldn't be a lot of trouble."

As Faye's request tumbled out in its roundabout way Abby's agreeable smile masked more than a little uncertainty. Small infants were her particular downfall. Unless she made a concerted effort not to respond to them at all, almost to the point of ignoring them, she couldn't resist cuddling them, although returning them to their mothers' arms always left her feeling bereft. But since Robert was sleeping, she would be far less tempted to pick him up and risk disturbing him. If she could avoid actually holding him close to her, she wouldn't be swamped with that feeling of utter vulnerability helpless babies invariably evoked in her.

She nodded at Faye. "Of course, I'll be glad to watch him for you."

"Bless your heart. I knew I could count on you. I'm sorry to have to bother you, since the two of you were just on your way out to play tennis."

"Your mother is a little more important than a game of tennis we can play anytime, so run along and take her to her doctor," Abby insisted, though a slight movement of her hand denoted some hesitancy. "If the baby cries, though, should I feed him, or what? I have to admit I don't have much experience with infants."

"I have a little," Joel spoke up wryly, taking Abby's tennis racket and propping it up with his beside the door, along with both cans of balls. "I'll help you with the baby. You can go, Faye. We'll be just fine."

"Never doubted it for a minute" was her reply as she flew up the stairs for a quick change of clothes.

As Abby preceded Joel into the living room she glanced once at the portable crib standing before the cold fireplace, then sank down into the first chair she came upon, quite aware that he went directly to the side of the crib. Her gaze followed him.

After looking down into the crib for a moment, Joel turned to Abby. "Sleeping like a baby," he pronounced dryly, unsuccessfully fighting a smile when Abby lifted her eyes heavenward at the worst pun she had heard in quite some time. "Okay, it was bad, but I never claimed to be a comedian."

"Good thing."

Still smiling, Joel reached down to pull the lightweight blanket farther back from the baby's face. "Nice looking kid. Have you seen him?"

"Umm, this morning, when Valerie brought him by," Abby said while scrupulously examining her fingernails. "He is a handsome little boy."

Returning from across the room, Joel settled himself comfortably on the sofa next to Abby's chair. "You said you haven't had much experience with small babies, but I thought almost all teenage girls did a lot of baby-sitting."

"I didn't do much at all. There just weren't many small children or babies in our neighborhood."

Joel leaned toward her, skimming a hand down her arm to take hold of hers and to play idly with her fingertips. "Do you realize I know very little about your childhood? You've mentioned your parents and your sister occasionally, but didn't you have any other relatives living in Chattanooga?"

"Most of Dad's family still live in Indiana, but my mother's parents and younger brother, Ted, lived close enough for us to see them often," Abby murmured, shifting restlessly in her chair before she produced an exceptionally cheery smile. "Why don't I get us some iced tea, or would you prefer coffee?"

After he chose the former, she went into the kitchen to pour tea freshly brewed for lunch from a cut-glass pitcher into two tall glasses filled with chunks of ice. On the rim of Joel's glass she placed a segment of lemon, then found a black-and-red enameled tray and carried the drinks back to the living room. She stopped short in the doorway, watching as Joel lifted the baby out of his crib.

"He woke up and kicked off his blanket," Joel explained when he turned and saw Abby. Then, with a clearly hopeful inflection in his deep voice, he added, "He's very wet."

Abby walked in, placed the tray on a side table, and went to him, giving him a cheeky grin. "I can take a hint and I understand perfectly. You can perform delicate surgery on a baby but have no idea how to go about putting on a diaper."

"Oh, I can do it. But since you're volunteering . . ."

"Put him back down, then," she instructed, lowering the side of the crib. As she proceeded to exchange the wet diaper for a dry one the wide-awake baby kicked, cooed a bit, and gave her several of those toothless bubbly smiles she could never resist. After his rubber pants were securely snapped on again and the blanket was around him, Abby picked the baby up and cuddled him close against her breasts. "There we go, Robert," she said softly, carrying him to the sofa, where she sat down beside Joel. "That's more comfortable, isn't it?"

Robert cooed again and kicked the ends of the blanket off his legs.

"He doesn't need that over him anyway. It's warm enough in here for him while he's awake and moving a little," Joel said. "And he doesn't seem the least bit sleepy."

Unable to drag her gaze away from Robert's round, chubby face and downy cap of hair, Abby nodded. "He wants some company. I noticed a rattle in his crib; maybe he'd like to wave that around."

"He's seems far too intrigued with your hair to be interested in any rattle." Smiling softly, Joel gently extracted a golden strand from a tightly clenched tiny fist. "Quite a grip. He must be pulling hard enough for it to hurt."

"It doesn't matter," Abby replied matter-of-factly.

As time passed Robert showed Abby and Joel his full repertoire of physical feats. Lying on his stomach, he could lift his head and survey his surroundings. Held against Abby's shoulder, he could thrust himself up on amazingly strong little legs, though his head did still bob a little with that maneuver. He was indeed intrigued by her shining hair, and she, in turn, was intrigued by him. The sweet clean scent of baby powder clung to his soft, finely textured skin, and his baby warmth radiated into her as she held him. With some shame she even felt rather reluctant to give the baby to Joel when it occurred to her he might wish to hold Robert also.

Watching Joel with Robert was a fascinating experience. His expertise with infants and his endearing gentleness were nearly mesmerizing, yet disturbing at the same time. Abby couldn't help feeling rather relieved when Robert started fretting as if he missed having her hair to play with. The moment Joel returned him to her waiting arms, he actually did stop fussing immediately and tangled tiny fingers in the forward-falling curtain of her hair.

"Oh, you do like that, don't you?" Abby gently stroked his cap of hair. "I like yours too but I'm not pulling it, so please don't tug so hard at mine." Almost as if he'd understood her words, the baby relaxed his grip, and she looked with delight at Joel. Her soft laughter was caught in her throat, however, when she saw the bright illumination in his dark eyes.

One large hand came up, and his sensitive fingertips traced ovals over the slightly heightened color in her cheeks. "You know what, Abby?" he whispered. "I think that someday you're going to be a terrific mother."

It was the worst thing in the world he could have said. The words stunned Abby as much as if she had been slapped in the face, but as they began to sink into her consciousness the initial blessed numbness gave way to a blazing core of pain that soon radiated throughout her chest. At her most vulnerable while holding another woman's baby in her arms, she felt on the verge of a deluge of tears because of Joel's innocent remark but fought against crying in front of him with every ounce of inner strength until the need to cry was subdued and confined deep in her heart. Before she had succeeded in suppressing that need, however, a few tears had misted her eyes and she lowered her head to conceal them from him, but not before noticing that his expression was now questioning.

Fortunately, Faye arrived home at that moment and diverted Joel's attention long enough for Abby to compose herself to some extent. Still, she felt an overpowering need to escape, to be alone for just a little while, and she stood immediately when Faye entered the living room.

"Oh, he's awake," the older woman exclaimed softly. "Oh, dear, has he given you much trouble—been terribly fussy?"

"Not at all," Abby said, feeling as if her cheeks would crack under the strain of a forced smile that she knew couldn't be at all convincing. After kissing Robert's fat cheeks lightly, she handed him to Faye, who hadn't yet even put her purse down. "He's a very good baby, in fact. He didn't cry once. And, my, isn't he exceptionally strong to only be eight weeks old?" She knew she was babbling on but couldn't stop as she glanced at Joel. "Could we

117

postpone our tennis game until later this afternoon? I've just remembered something I must do. Excuse me, I'll be upstairs."

Abby restrained from dashing out of the room and maintained a slow, steady pace across the hall. As she climbed the stairs she heard Faye's voice, then Joel's deeper tones, but their words were indistinguishable. She moved quietly across the upstairs gallery, and although most of her belongings had been transferred by then into Joel's room, it wasn't his door she opened. Instead, she entered the bedroom next to his, the one Faye had given her upon her arrival at Fairfields. She closed the door behind her. She walked woodenly to the center of the room, then stopped and simply stood there for moments that seemed to stretch into an eternity.

Joel's words "I think that someday you're going to be a terrific mother" replayed like a broken record in her mind until she knew they must be branded on her brain. A throbbing ache attacked her temples but was nothing compared to the raw pain in her chest. She should have cried then but wouldn't, characteristically refusing to vent emotions already kept strictly in check for too long. Despite near Herculean self-control, she was unable to silence Joel's ceaselessly repeating words. Desperate to think about anything else, she pressed fingertips against her forehead and glanced around the room, producing an audible sound of relief when she noticed her briefcase on the vanity chair, papers spilling half out of it—papers she had hardly glanced at since her arrival.

Work. She would throw herself into her work for a couple of hours. That would help. Besides enjoying what she did, she had learned long ago that work also provided an escape. And there had only been a couple of other times in her life when she needed to escape as much as she needed to at that moment.

Even so, she realized she couldn't hope to concentrate

yet. Her fingers fumbled with the zipper of her tennis skirt but she finally lowered it, dropped the skirt carelessly down around her feet, then stepped out of it while pulling the red-and-white sleeveless cotton jersey over her head. Stripped to her undergarments, she remembered her sneakers, untied them, kicked them off, and went into the adjoining bathroom, intending to take the hottest shower she could bear.

Steam was already fogging the mirror when Abby tested the water temperature with one hand, then bravely stepped backward, gasping as the hot spray peppered her back. With the water as hot as she could stand it, she lathered her entire body, and by the time she rinsed the soap away the heat had melted some of her physical tension away. Simply making herself endure the stinging spray required concentration, and thus the debilitating train of thought she had sought to escape did lose some of its impetus . . . but only for a minute or two.

With a suddenness that made Abby's heart skip a beat, the sliding opaque glass shower door was pushed aside, and Joel stood outside the enclosure in the swirling steam, his stony eyes raking over her before settling on her face.

"*Joel!* What—" Abby stammered, surprise rendering her motionless. "For goodness sake, I'm taking a shower."

"That's fairly obvious," he snapped, his hands thrust deep in his pockets as he took an oddly menacing step closer. "Abby, what the hell— What happened downstairs to make you leave the way you did, as if you couldn't get away from Faye and me fast enough?"

"Nothing happened," she lied. "What gave you the impression—"

"*You* gave us the impression. Oh, you said all the right things, but the closed expression on your face completely shut us out. It was so obvious you couldn't wait to get away from us that Faye thought maybe you were upset with her for asking you to watch the baby."

119

Genuine regret made Abby flinch. She shook her head emphatically. "Oh, I'm sorry she thought that, because it certainly isn't true. And as soon as I've finished my shower I'll go down and tell her that."

"You'll have to wait. It was time to take Robert home to his mother, so Faye's just driven away," Joel ground out, his jaw clenched. The expression tightening his features lost none of its harshness even as his gaze dropped down to follow the path of the water splashing over her shoulders to run in rivulets over full creamy caramel-tipped breasts and lower. His sensuously shaped lips compressed to a grim line. "And is this what you absolutely had to do—take a damn shower? This was more important to you than being civil to Faye and playing tennis with me?"

"I *was* civil! Don't you tell me I wasn't," Abby protested, the tears springing to her eyes mercifully indistinguishable from the droplets of water that splattered her face. She *knew* she had been civil to Faye and to him; knew she had done everything in her power to act as if nothing were the matter, although her heart had felt it was being ripped open by the words that *he* had said. Then, he was up there accusing her of not being civil, and she wasn't going to let him tear her emotions into even tinier shreads. Her blue eyes stormy gray then, she wiped at the water splashing over the right side of her jaw and running down her neck. "And if you must know, I didn't come up here just to have a shower. I came to look over some data I'll be using for my advertising campaign presentation, because, after all, I haven't done much work in four or five days."

"To hell with your work," he muttered, reaching into the shower, careless that his muscular, hair-roughened arms were drenched as he grasped the faucets and shut off the flow of water. With the abrupt silencing of the forceful spray, an ominous quiet filled the small closed room. His eyes were like shards of dark ice impaling hers. "Even if

120

you do have work on your mind, you can't keeping going hot and cold on people all the time. And if you're really telling me the truth and nothing's actually bothering you, and the way you act can be attributed to sudden changes of mood, then I'm telling you now, Abby, I'm getting very bored with your damn moodiness."

"*Are you really?*" she snapped back, hurt flaring into a defensive anger and a need to lash back at him. "You've always known about my moods, but you didn't seem very bored with me on the boat after the ball and you haven't seemed bored during the days and nights since, either."

"You could try the patience of a saint," he uttered after cursing beneath his breath. He gripped her upper arms and pinioned them against her sides. "I'd like to take you out of there and— But never mind, I wouldn't think of keeping you from your work. I'll go for a drive instead, and you'll have the whole house to yourself. You can slave away to your heart's content."

Out of the turmoil of conflicting emotions roiling within Abby love for Joel emerged stronger than all the rest, love accompanied by the fear of letting him go away as angry as he was, plus a deeper, even more dreadful fear that if he went, she might lose even the fragile, tenuous relationship they then shared. It was love combined with those fears that made her move, made her catch hold of his hands as they abruptly dropped from her arms.

"Joel, wait," she whispered urgently. "Why are we fighting? Downstairs, I never meant to make you and Faye think I wanted to get away from you. I just— Don't be angry. And don't leave. Stay with me. I don't want to work now. I only want you."

Joel's groan was low and rough as Abby stepped out of the shower enclosure and pressed against him, slender arms going around his neck. He held her away for a moment, his dark eyes glinting with passion and devouring every inch of her invitingly bare, water-glistened body.

He undid the towel she had twisted into a turban on her head and, as her hair tumbled down in a golden cascade over his hand, his lean fingers tangled in silken strands.

"*Abby,* are you trying to drive me crazy?" he whispered back huskily. Molding her entrancingly curved frame to the lithe length of his, uncaring that the water on her satiny skin soaked through the fabric of his tennis shorts and shirt, he tilted her head back, cradling it in one hand, as his mouth came down with potent power to take possession of her softly parted lips.

Abby melted into him, kissing him back, prepared for this, the proper precautions taken as they had always been taken since the day they had sailed back to Fairfields on the *Sea Nymph.* Because she had known how swiftly and easily passion could flare between them, she had also known she must always be ready for this eventuality. And it was without hesitation that she wrapped her arms tightly around his strong neck, loving the feel of her taut, throbbing breasts yielding to his hard chest. The buttons of his shirt pressed into her warm flesh, and she slipped a hand between him and herself to begin unfastening them.

"*Abby,* you smell so sweet, so delicious, I could devour you," Joel said, sending a thrill like an electric shock rushing through her as he gently caught between his teeth the tender curve of her lower lip. "You taste delicious. I *need* you."

"Take me to bed," she breathed against his hard marauding mouth. "Now, Joel."

Reaching behind him for the large bath towel she had laid out, he wrapped it around her and, swooping her up in his arms as if she weighed nothing at all, strode from the bath and across her room to the wide canopied bed. He put her down to remove his sneakers and clothes and, as she lifted her arms to him, he lowered himself gently on top of her before turning onto his side and taking her into his arms. He buried his face in the thickness of her faintly perfumed hair as she pressed closer and closer against his strong thighs.

"You *are* driving me crazy," he muttered, his breath warm and caressing in her ear. "What am I going to do with you?"

"Love me. Love me, love me," she answered, her own love and need for him overcoming all inhibitions as she touched him, caressed him, kissed him.

His mouth plundered her lips. His hands swept over her, following every enticing curve and sending a lightning-quick blaze over every inch of her skin. As mutual passion burned out of control in the tangle of bedclothes, their limbs became entangled, and Abby's soft bemused gaze was held by the burning light of Joel's. He moved above her, his hand beneath her hips, uplifting, and they watched each other as their bodies merged perfectly.

"Oh, yes, Joel," she uttered ecstatically, her fingers entwining in the thick dark hair on his nape as her mouth sought his. They began to move together, and she cried out silently, *Make me forget. Make me forget everything except you and this.*

And, as always, for a long time, he did.

CHAPTER EIGHT

"Come see these," Joel said softly. Taking Abby by the hand, he led her around a freshly painted white column, up one step, and into a small alcove where several refreshing, vibrant seascapes were arranged.

After viewing an endless array of typical ocean scenes, watercolors in which pale hues merged drearily into one another to become blurred pictures lacking natural lines and life, that collection in the alcove was indeed an invigorating find. The canvases by J. Earl, who had signed them in tiny letters in a lower corner, were vigorously alive, the lines clear and true to life and the colors natural, some strikingly bright, some dull, some in between, but never blurred, as if J. Earl viewed nature long distance through acutely farsighted eyes.

"We always find something terrific in this gallery," Abby said, smiling up at Joel. "We may have to endure several mediocre collections, but we always discover one like this. Oh, I love all these paintings and I have a feeling the unknown J. Earl won't be unknown for long. Some of Old Charleston's most pretentious little galleries might be fighting to show his work soon."

Joel nodded. "I think you might be right. The use of shadow and light in these paintings makes for striking realism. And have you noticed that there's not one of a wave crashing against jagged rocks?"

"And not *one* of disintegrating wood pilings leaning over a pool of turgid water," Abby added with delight. "It's truly amazing."

"There's not even one of a couple of stalks of sea oats sticking out of a sand dune."

"Or one of an old boat deserted on the beach."

"This J. Earl is obviously an original thinker," Joel said, slipping an arm around Abby's waist as they examined more closely the first canvas. "I think I'd like to have one of these. You help me decide which one."

"I like them all," she said, and it was true. Her attention, however, strayed almost immediately from the first canvas to the next painting, one of a sun-washed cove that very much resembled the cove where she and Joel had anchored the *Sea Nymph*. The scene was so lifelike that she felt drawn into it and she found herself yearning for the painting in a way she rarely yearned for material things. Its price was fairly high but not prohibitive, and she decided she might buy it.

After they had viewed the entire collection, Joel stood back from it to survey the paintings individually, thoughtfully stroking his jaw before glancing at Abby. "Have you picked a favorite? Several of them really appeal to me."

"If you buy several, I'm sure J. Earl will be delighted," she told him, smiling as she gestured toward the second canvas. "But my favorite is the one of the cove. I like the way the sunlight—"

"Abby. Abby, hi," a soft, drawling feminine voice interrupted. "It's a surprise seeing you here. You are on vacation, aren't you? I thought you'd gone out of town."

Abby smiled a welcome as Vicky Kittredge stepped up into the alcove, automatically smoothing her perpetually rumpled chestnut hair, which she claimed was the bane of her existence.

"Yes, I'm on vacation," Abby told the newcomer. "Staying out at Fairfields, so I guess you can't really consider that going out of town."

"Well, it's a long drive in, so I understand why you didn't make Monday night's meeting at the Foundation. We missed you, though," Vicky said, turning to Joel as if to graciously include him in the conversation. "Abby's been such a terrific worker since she volunteered to help the Foundation. We all—"

"Oh, excuse me, let me introduce you two," Abby interrupted as casually as possible. "Vicky Kittredge, Dr. Joel Richmond."

"*The* Dr. Joel Richmond? The pediatric surgeon?" Vicky inquired, the swift uplifting of her brows indicating she was clearly impressed when Joel nodded. She smiled warmly at him. "Well, I am so pleased to make your acquaintance. I've heard a great deal about you, of course, and all of it good."

Joel smiled back just as warmly. "Thank you. And I've heard a great many good words spoken about you, Mrs. Kittredge. Most Charlestonians know how dedicated you are to several worthwhile causes."

"We all have our duties in this world. I feel I fulfill mine best in volunteerism," Vicky said sincerely, incapable of affectation. "And do please call me Vicky, and I'll call you Joel. Now, Joel, as I was saying, Abby has helped the Foundation so much. Before she volunteered, we were having a devil of a time getting publicity. But she's been working so hard for us, and with her advertising experience we're having very little trouble publicizing now, especially our fund-raising events. And it's all Abby's doing. I declare, sometimes I think she's a miracle worker."

"Really, Vicky, you do much more than I do," Abby said softly, blushing slightly at the genuine, but rather

126

grandiose, praise. Feeling Joel's gaze on her, she looked up at him, a certain uneasiness stealing over her when she saw the disturbed and disturbing expression on his dark face.

"It's nice to hear Abby's such a help to you," he said as he turned his attention exclusively to Vicky again. "And exactly which foundation is this?"

"Oh, Vicky, I didn't tell you the good news yet, did I?" Abby asked, the words rushing out before the older woman could even begin to answer Joel's question. "I've persuaded a printer I know to donate his time and materials to make up the posters announcing our next benefit. Isn't that kind of him?"

"My, yes, indeed it is. You must give me his name and address so I can send him a personal note of thanks." With Joel's question mercifully forgotten, Vicky glanced at her diamond-and-gold wristwatch, then stilled Abby's hand as she brought pen and paper from her straw purse. "Give that information to me the very next time I see you, honey, because now I really do have to run to a meeting. I just dropped in here for a second. I try to come as often as I can, since this is one of the pitifully few galleries in town that will show work by people who really aren't known." For the first time she really looked around the alcove and was pleasantly surprised. "Now, these are fine, aren't they? Goodness, I wish I didn't have to run. Maybe I can drop back by here again tomorrow and have a longer look at them." Still talking as if to herself, she descended the one step and waved jauntily back over one shoulder. "See you all later."

As Vicky departed, her footfalls purposefully tapping across the gallery's wooden floor, Abby turned to Joel, smiling. "She's a wonderful woman. And sometimes endearingly funny, the way she talks to herself."

"She is very nice. I liked her," Joel concurred, even as he took Abby's elbow and guided her into a shadowed corner of the alcove. His hands spanned her waist, quite

127

blatantly imprisoning her between the back wall and himself. "Tell me a little more about all this, Abby. For instance, you could start by telling me which foundation you do volunteer work for."

Abby gazed up at him. For a fleeting instant there was something so compelling in his dark eyes, in his low tone, and even in the seemingly tensed contours of his body that nearly made her tell exactly which foundation it was. Then her heart began to race and she couldn't do it. The fear was too intense. Certain she would suffer if he ever guessed the truth, she was unable even to tell him she did work for the Hemophilia Foundation. She was unreasonably afraid that one word would somehow arouse his suspicions.

Even as she mentally accused herself of being almost ridiculously overcautious, she thought of another of Vicky's worthwhile causes. She named it, and was able to breathe more easily when Joel readily accepted what she told him.

"I had no idea you were involved in any volunteer work since you stopped spending your Saturdays in the pediatrics ward at the medical center," he said quietly, moving a little closer as his penetrating gaze explored her uptilted face. "But then, I'm continually learning things about you, it seems. Why won't you ever tell me very much about yourself?"

"Mainly because there's so very little to tell," Abby responded, her light laugh trying to dismiss his question entirely. "I mean, it just never occurred to me to mention doing volunteer work at the Foundation, because doing it certainly doesn't make me an unusual person. Millions of people serve as volunteers every day."

"That's not the point. The point I'm trying to make is that your doing volunteer work is just another thing I didn't know about you. It certainly makes me wonder what else I don't know."

128

"I can't think of anything else."

"Maybe *you* can't, but I've gotten to the point where it really wouldn't surprise me for someone to tell me you'd been chosen to represent the United States in the high jump competition at the next Olympics."

"Well, you needn't worry," Abby said wryly. "No one's ever going to tell you that."

"That's a relief," he replied, light fingers lifting a stray wisp of golden hair from where it grazed her cheek to brush it back from her face. "I'd hate to think you would keep news like that a secret from me."

"I'm going to say something now that isn't news and certainly is no secret," Abby murmured, choosing to respond to the half-teasing note in his deep voice rather than the half-serious one. Taking a step nearer, she laid her hands against his chest. "And what I have to say is that right this minute we're only about five blocks from my apartment."

"That's a fact I'm well aware of," Joel answered, a smile tugging at the corners of his mouth. "And if that's an invitation . . ."

"It is."

"I accept. But what about those two charming spinster sisters you rent from? If we lock ourselves away in your place in the middle of the afternoon, they could be so shocked by your wanton behavior, they might evict you."

"I happen to know that Miss Stella and Miss Mallie are attending their regular-as-clockwork sewing circle this afternoon. And when that's over, they'll take each other out to dinner. They always do," Abby whispered conspiratorially, then laughed. "Besides, you'd be surprised how very little shocks those two ladies. They may be elderly spinsters, but they watch all the soap operas and tell me they find them very enlightening, if not downright educational."

Joel chuckled. "Then we couldn't possibly shock them

129

if we tried, so we'll go to your place after we buy what we want here." He and Abby turned their attention back to the collection of paintings. "You liked the one of the cove. Going to buy it?"

"I'm not sure," Abby said, thoughtfully nibbling a nail, then glancing curiously at him. "Why do you ask? If I decide not to take it, will you?"

"If you don't want it. . . ."

"You have it," she insisted, inwardly delighted that he liked that particular painting too, although she couldn't be sure it was because it actually reminded him of *their* cove.

Ten minutes later, after Joel had paid the gallery owner for three J. Earl paintings and had them put aside to be picked up later, he and Abby stepped outside into the bright afternoon sunshine and started toward Market Street. For her, with her hand securely clasped in his, their stroll through Old Charleston evoked a great many lovely memories of all the other long walks they had taken together before she had realized she could have no future with him. But that was past and this was present, and when Joel suddenly leaned down his dark head and lightly kissed her lips, then smiled unabashedly at the passersby on the narrow sidewalk, she found a true joy in that moment, a joy she had no intention of relinquishing until she had no other choice.

"It's been quite some time since I've walked through here," Joel noted as they turned a corner and left Market for another street also lined with lovely old southern mansions. "Not since the last time I came with you."

"I haven't really walked here since then either. No time," Abby told him, though that wasn't strictly true. In actuality, she simply hadn't been able to endure the thought of going there without him. But at that moment he was with her once more, and that in itself accentuated the loveliness of the stately old homes that rose straight up near the sidewalk. Small enclosed gardens released a potpourri of fragrances into the air and these mingled with the scent of the leaves of the crape myrtles, their boughs occasionally arcing over the tops of walls, burgeoning with emerging buds of pink or white. Sunlight filtering through the branches played in dappled patterns on the walk and brought a dreamy smile to Abby's lips. "This really is a beautiful area."

"We missed most of the spring here," Joel commented expressionlessly. "That's usually considered the prettiest time of year in Charleston."

"Oh, it was lovely. I didn't walk here then, but I enjoyed driving through on my way back and forth to work."

They walked on in silence then, but it wasn't a strained one as they turned at another corner, then one more, until they were on the street where Abby lived. The antebellum homes that lined the sidewalk there couldn't be considered mansions, but what they lacked in size they more than made up for in quaintness, quiet dignity, and charm. On the right, near the center of the block, Misses Mallie and Stella Taylor's residence of cream stucco, accented by black shutters and vibrantly colored flowers spilling from the window boxes, drew the discerning eye. Upon approaching it, Abby never failed to feel fortunate that she had been able to rent the entire second floor of the two sisters' narrow house.

When Joel swung open the wrought-iron gate to the diminutive side garden, Abby preceded him along the short brick path to the stairs that led up to a tiny balcony and her own private entrance to her apartment. Joel took the key she extracted from her purse, unlocked the French doors, then followed when she entered the high-ceilinged, yet cozy, sitting room. As Abby opened windows to allow fresh air to replace the stale odor that had accumulated during her absence, she noticed out of the corner of her eye that Joel appeared to be as at home there as he once had been . . . and as she once had been in his house.

Excusing herself for a moment, she left the room and went down the hall to open windows in her bedroom and in the kitchen in back, where a tapestry screen attractively formed a dining area.

When she returned to the sitting room, she found Joel standing behind the sofa, looking around.

"You've rearranged things," he commented. "And added a few new pieces, I see."

Abby smiled. "You're very observant. I have bought some things since you were here last."

He gestured toward the mahogany secretary across from him, its simple lines in keeping with the other furnishings. "I like that. Antique?"

"Heavens, no." Amusement danced in her eyes at the very thought. "You, Doctor, may be wealthy enough to afford genuine period antiques, but I have to settle for reproductions. The only genuine articles here are the candlesticks on the mantel, the glass-domed anniversary clock, which, by the way, is still incredibly accurate, and a few of the other tiny accessory items."

"Reproductions or not, they make the room elegant but comfortable at the same time. I compliment you, my dear, on your excellent taste in decorating."

"I do thank you kindly, sir," Abby responded, exaggerating her drawl and curtsying low. She smiled at him. "How about a drink? Scotch and water or gin and tonic?"

"Gin and tonic."

Nodding, she turned to leave him again, calling back over her shoulder as she stepped out into the hall, "Make yourself comfortable. I won't be long."

Joel took her at her word, as she discovered a few minutes later when she returned with his drink and a glass of white wine for herself. During her absence he had removed his navy linen blazer, unfastened another button of his shirt, and was now settled on the sofa, his long legs extended in front of him, his hands clasped at the back of

132

his head, and his eyes closed. When she walked across the room toward him, however, he opened them to intently watch her approach. As always, such an appraising observation by him made her heart beat a little faster and brought a tinge of rose color to her cheeks from excitement strangely edged by a hint of shyness. She met his inscrutable gaze directly, though, as she handed him his drink, then sat down on the sofa beside him.

After a small sip of chilled wine, she inquired, "Did I hear you telling Faye we might stay in town to have dinner?"

"Yes, I told her that," Joel said, surveying her over the rim of the glass he had just raised to his lips. "Why?"

"Oh, I just . . . well, we *could* dine out. Or we could order something to eat here. Or we could go buy . . . maybe fresh shrimp and prepare them ourselves."

Joel's eyes narrowed as he took a swallow of his drink, then lowered the glass. "Shrimp boiled in beer and bay leaves? Like we used to have them?"

"Yes, like that."

The edge of Joel's forefinger grazed the underside of Abby's small chin, and while his thumb pressed down lightly over it he lifted her head up and turned her to face him. "Sounds delicious," he said softly. "Is the market we always went to still open until nine at night?"

"I'm sure it is."

"Good. We don't have to rush right out, then."

"No, we don't have to rush at all," she murmured, beginning to lose herself in the dark depths of his eyes. "We have the rest of the afternoon and the early evening."

"For what, Abby?"

"For anything we want," she answered, aware of the slight warming of her cheeks. "For sitting, talking, relaxing."

"Or for whatever else we might want?"

133

Abby took another sip of wine, then nodded. "Yes, for whatever else."

They did sit and talk for quite awhile, and Abby was totally relaxed when, after they finished their drinks, Joel put his arms around her, turned her, and brought her around to him until she was half reclining on his muscular thighs. He cradled her against him, stroking a hand over her shining hair, and the expression that lay over his carved features was tenderly sensuous. When she reached up to draw her fingertips over the hard contour and smooth plane of his right cheek, he smiled slowly down at her. And when she smiled back at him, he lowered his head until his lips hovered just above her own. Then they touched hers, strong and firm, yet exquisitely gentle in brushing them apart, playing over their softness.

For a long spellbinding time they exchanged kisses that were fulfilling in themselves. Joel's strong hands moved over Abby's back and waist while her smaller ones caressed his chest. It was a lovely languid time of preliminary touching that Abby gloried in and in which Joel too seemed to find deep satisfaction. When he lazily tasted the warmth of her mouth, and her tongue just as lazily grazed the edge of his, he murmured his pleasure and held her closer to him but confined his hands still to the delicate probing of her waist and back. Between the lengthening kisses they whispered endearments, and once he slightly lifted his head to say softly, "Abby, it's been such a long time since we spent an afternoon in this room doing this."

"I know," she whispered back, wondering what he would think if she told him exactly how long it *had* been, if she told him the precise number of months, weeks, and days. Her heart seemed to have acquired the knack for keeping track of the time, almost to the hours and minutes, that had gone by since it had all ended between them. But then he was kissing her again, and she was kissing him

134

back. She didn't tell him and knew deep down inside that it was better that she didn't.

Abby moved slightly in Joel's embrace, turning closer toward him, one arm gliding up around his shoulders, the firmly rounded swells of her breasts pliable against him. With a swiftness that quickened and made more keen the sensations inside her, their kiss deepened and flowered and became a promise of ecstasy to come. As his arms brought her more tightly against him, she became even more warmly yielding, her body simmering in a rush of aroused femininity, and entrancingly cushioned flesh and bone sought closer contact with him. Her thighs curved around his side as she clasped her arms around his neck and raised herself a little to more ardently receive and return his kisses.

A whispery moan of delight escaped Abby's parted lips, which submitted softly to the firm line of Joel's as he claimed their lush tenderness. And when his pleasantly rough fingertips slid beneath one wide strap of her sundress to ease it off her shoulder and nuzzled his face against fresh-scented, silken-textured, and hotly sensitized skin, Abby showered light kisses over the rapid steady pulse in his throat.

With lips warm and seeking, Joel made daring little forays across her shoulder and down across her delicately structured collarbone. The flicking of the tip of his tongue into the hollow at the base of her slender neck made her tremble, and he trembled too when she rubbed a hand down over his chest to unbutton his shirt. Her hand eased beneath the cloth. Her fingers traced the muscular contours of his heated male flesh. Her nails caught and tugged gently at his fine dark hair, and his passion erupted in a blaze of fire that could no longer be even temporarily controlled. Hoarsely saying her name, he pushed off the other strap of her dress and brushed the bodice lower, exposing the curving flesh of her breasts to the evocative exploration of his mouth and softly nibbling teeth.

Abby lay back in his arms, her senses spiraling in rising desire, lost in the sheer delight of his caresses. She swept her fingers through his hair, breathlessly acquiescent when he raised her up just enough to pull down the back zipper of her dress. Turning her head, she trailed her lips over his chest, exulting in his clean male scent and the magnitude of physical power that she sensed he was now only scarcely able to restrain.

Joel curved one hand around Abby's neck and, with his thumb, urgently lifted her chin for the strong seducing descent of his warm mouth onto her eagerly awaiting lips. They clung to each other, their bodies fitting together as perfectly as matching puzzle pieces.

He released her lips only to murmur close to her ear, "It's been so long since we made love in your bed, Abby."

"Too long," she whispered back. She eased his shirt completely off his shoulder, and with her touch, his corded muscles rippled beneath her fingertips. "Much too long."

He held her appealingly small face in one cupped hand, looking down at her. A burning glow in the depths of his seductive brown eyes denoted both passion and tenderness. His slow smile was sensuous. "We're very good together," he said softly, kissing her eyebrows, the tip of her nose, and the high bones of her porcelain-smooth cheeks. "And what we have together is right. You know that, don't you, Abby?"

"*Yes.* Yes, I know," she answered breathlessly, because it was true. What they had together *was* right. Although she harbored a major secret and its growing entourage of minor secrets that she dared not share with him, she could still give herself physically without reservations, without inhibitions, and take back from him. Because of her need to give, such a consuming force in her, it was undeniably right that she give herself to him.

136

CHAPTER NINE

Two afternoons later Abby and Joel sat on a bench in a secluded bower in the gardens at Fairfields. Rosebushes surrounded them, some bearing yellow blossoms, some red, some ivory, some pink, plus others of a myriad of shades in between. An occasional soft breeze played through the green leaves and stirred up the roses' combined fragrances, wafting them through the air. It was that lazy kind of do-nothing day that even seemed to mute the buzzing of the bees as they winged lethargically from bloom to bloom. Birdsong was heard infrequently from the trees, and Abby could imagine the feathered creatures dozing on leaf-canopied branches, because she too felt increasingly drowsy with Joel's arm around her and her head resting comfortably in the hollow of his shoulder.

Her eyelids were becoming heavier and heavier, and it was no wonder. She and Joel had spent most of the morning cavorting on the beach. After lunch, they played tennis, and afterward, when they had emerged from their showers, both of them had logically desired to spend the remainder of the afternoon simply lounging around. And when Joel suggested they find some secluded corner of the gardens in which to sit quietly, Abby had hidden a yawn behind one hand and nodded agreeably.

Losing the battle with her weighted eyelids, Abby now allowed them to close and soon drifted into that pleasant state between wakefulness and sleep. Satisfied that the slower rate of the rise and fall of Joel's chest meant he too was dozing, she smiled to herself, and the smile still curved her lips after she had fallen asleep.

Sometime later voices from a distance partially roused Abby, but because she heard in them a predominantly childlike treble, she thought she must be merely emerging from a dream. Then she realized the voices were drawing nearer, sounding louder, and she knew she and Joel were no longer alone in the gardens—not that it mattered. But as she started to press her cheek more comfortably against Joel's pillowing shoulder, a child's laughter elicited her attention. She sat up straight, suddenly wide awake, delight dancing in her aqua eyes and illuminating her face. Quietly calling Joel's name, she laid a hand on his arm and gently shook it. His eyes opened at once, a conditioned reflex from his days as an intern, but before Abby could tell him what was happening, he saw for himself.

With boisterous enthusiasm the two Howard children careened into the shady bower, Davy, the four-year-old, darting ahead of his sister, Ellie, only two and a half. Although she let go with a howl of angry protest, he ignored her as if she didn't exist and ran on to propel himself toward Abby.

A big boy for his age, he landed squarely on Abby's lap, but she didn't mind being slightly squashed. Laughing, she hugged him to her. "My, you're growing so fast, Davy, that soon you're going to be as tall as your father," she told him fondly while reaching one arm around him to take hold of Ellie's small hand, drawing her closer. Needing no more encouragement than that, the auburn-haired little girl scrambled onto the bench beside Abby and wrapped her plump little arms around Abby's neck. Abby hugged her tight in one arm while rumpling Davy's hair with her free hand as she murmured, "Is that a new dress you're wearing, Ellie? You sure look pretty in it."

Ellie's response was happy bubbling laughter, then she and Davy turned their attention to Joel, whom they didn't know quite as well as they knew Abby but liked very much nevertheless. After Joel solemnly shook the hand Davy proudly thrust out, he reached for Ellie, and she went confidently into his arms to bestow a very sweet, if somewhat damp, kiss on his cheek.

"Can't children take a nice peaceful afternoon and turn it upside down?" Faye asked with a grin as she strolled into the bower, love for her children warming her eyes. She lifted her hands and rolled her eyes heavenward for Joel's and Abby's amusement. "Guess who got homesick staying with Grandma and Grandpa Howard and absolutely had to be brought back to Mama and Daddy today?"

"Was it Davy?" Abby asked, squeezing his hand as she played out the guessing game. "Or was it Ellie?"

When both children looked then at their mother with totally bland, innocent expressions on their faces, the three adults had to laugh at their charming expertise in the art of not looking guilty. It is an art every child learns early and easily, but these two were particularly talented at it.

"Since they'll never tell, I will," Faye said at last, still chuckling. "*Both* of them were homesick, actually. And I have to admit I was beginning to really miss them, too."

"You don't have to tell Abby and me that," Joel drawled, his smile etching attractive creases beside his mouth. "We know you insisted on keeping Valerie's baby the other day mainly because Ellie and Davy weren't here."

"You know, that's exactly what David said, and both

of you are right. The house was just beginning to seem so empty without the kids around," Faye admitted, then moved her lips into a little moue. "I swear, though, it's terrible when just about everyone you know can tell what you're thinking. Sometimes I believe I must wear my heart on my sleeve."

"There's nothing wrong with letting other people know how you feel," Joel told her fondly. "You're just a very open, forthright person, Faye."

Unlike Abby, he seemed to be adding silently, but Abby pretended not to notice his subtly suggestive tone. Instead, she encouraged Davy to count from one to twenty, which he was pleased and proud to do. He counted loudly, claiming the attention of everyone except, unfortunately, his little sister, who was too young to appreciate his accomplishment. She began to fidget on Joel's lap until he fished his keys from his pocket and allowed her to flip them over one by one on the ring.

"Heavens, they're both sitting still at the same time. That's unusual, and if you two don't mind, I'll take advantage of it for a few minutes," Faye said. "I would like to call David at his office to tell him about his parents bringing the children home. I won't be long, okay?"

After both Abby and Joel had assured Faye that they would be glad to watch Davy and Ellie, and she had started back toward the house, Ellie almost immediately lost interest in the set of keys. She slipped off Joel's lap, tugged at his hand, and told him as best she could, in the language of a two-and-a-half-year-old, that she wanted to show him a bed of flowers she had planted herself.

"See mine, too," Davy said, hopping off the bench to pull at Abby's arms. "Mama helped her, but I planted mine all by myself."

A couple of minutes later Abby and Joel were able to quite honestly admire two separate sets of triple rows of scarlet gladiolas, each plant a sturdy green stalk bearing a multitude of alternating blossoms. Their sincere praise made both children beam, and Davy was actually strutting when the four started back toward the bower where Faye would expect to find them. While Joel slowed to a snail's pace because Ellie was inclined to dawdle along the paths, Abby had to quicken hers a bit to keep up with Davy. Following him along the winding path, she smiled lovingly at his long purposeful strides, which obviously made him feel very grown up. Both he and his sister meant a great deal to her. Perhaps because they were no longer helpless infants, they didn't arouse all of her latent maternal instincts as small babies did. She could simply love them as an aunt would, without wishing futilely and hurtfully that they were her own children.

Looking back at Abby as she followed him toward the bower, Davy grinned. "I learned to skip, did ya know? Watch, I'll show you."

With unusually good coordination for a child of four Davy skipped farther ahead of Abby into the shaded bower. "That's really very good," she called after him, then gasped as he suddenly misstepped and pitched forward with a cry of alarm.

Abby couldn't reach him in time to prevent the fall but arrived at his side only a second or so after he sprawled on the ground beside the bench. Already he was struggling to sit up, and as Abby gently helped him, she realized how narrowly he had missed striking his head on the corner of the marble bench top. Relief surged through her even after she turned him around in her arms and saw that his upper left arm had scraped the corner, resulting in a hopefully superficial scratch about two inches long. Though the scratch was bleeding somewhat, she knew a blow to the head would have been far more serious.

"Oh, dear, you've scraped your arm, but we'll soon fix that," she murmured reassuringly. "Does it hurt much, honey?"

141

"It's bleeding," he muttered, bravely trying not to cry, though tears were filling his big brown eyes. "Bad."

"No, not bad, just a little, and that's good because it helps clean everything out," she explained calmly while producing a folded fresh white handkerchief from the pocket of her denim skirt. Cradling Davy in her arms, she tenderly pressed the folded square over the injury and smiled down. "That better now?"

Although Davy nodded, he didn't seem particularly convinced. His chin wobbled and a few tears overflowed to dampen his cheeks when he saw Joel and Ellie enter the bower.

Assessing the situation immediately, Joel strode over to them, shaking his head sympathetically but giving the little boy a confident smile. "What's this, an accident? Did you fall down and hurt your arm?"

Careful not to sound the least bit excited, so Davy wouldn't become even more upset, Abby explained how the injury had occurred while Joel helped her, with the boy still in her arms, up onto the bench, where he knelt down before them. While he lifted the handkerchief to examine the wound Abby cradled the child's head against her breast, stroking his still-baby-fine hair and softly talking to him.

"Hmm" was Joel's only vocal reaction to what he saw, that typical physician's noncommittal response. He replaced the handkerchief and lightly pressed Abby's fingers over it again, then rose lithely to his feet. "Just hold that on there. I'll get my bag from the car. You stay here with Abby, Ellie."

When Joel had left the three in the bower, Ellie slowly sidled toward the bench, her big eyes transfixed on her older brother. She stepped up closer to him, then lifted her skirt a little to better show Abby the nearly faded evidence of a scraped knee.

"Oh, you fell down too, but it's all better now, isn't it?"

Abby gave the children a comforting smile. "Everybody falls down once in a while. Why, just the other day when your daddy was playing softball I saw him go ker-*plop* right down in the sand, so you see, anybody can fall."

Her deliberate emphasis on the nonsense word elicited a tiny smile even from Davy, and his eyes were dry again by the time Joel returned to kneel in front of the bench. Abby saw that the scratch began bleeding again as soon as Joel removed the handkerchief. Though she was afraid the cut might be deeper and more serious than she had originally thought, she gave no indication of her worry as she smiled back down at Davy. She did have to share the boy's wince as tears sparkled in his eyes once more when he saw the bottle of antiseptic Joel removed from his bag along with a sterile cottonball. Even little Ellie, who had moved aside, pulled down the skirt of her dress and expressed heartfelt commiseration for her brother in her wide solemn eyes.

"This will sting," Joel told Davy honestly while saturating the cotton. "But not for long. And you know I have to put this on to make the scratch better, don't you?"

As he spoke quietly to divert the child's attention and thus avoid a building dread, he applied the antiseptic-soaked cotton to the cut and thoroughly cleansed it.

In moments of crisis there are often final straws. For Davy, the application of the antiseptic was his. He sniffled, tears flowed, and he burrowed his wet face against Abby's neck. She stroked his back and murmured words of comfort while Joel also applied antiseptic salve and a light bandage. When the procedure was finished, Davy turned his head just enough to peek warily at Joel, who gave him an understanding smile and rumpled his hair. Davy almost smiled back until Faye stepped into the bower, a concerned frown knitting her brow when she took in the scene, and the slight upturning of the child's lips reversed

143

to a swift downcurving. His sobs began afresh in his need of the comfort only a mother can give.

Joel quickly explained the situation as Faye hurried to her son, hugged him close, and murmured, "Bless your heart."

"B'ess your heart." Ellie solemnly echoed her mother's words and received a smile from everyone except Davy, though Faye soon had him smiling, too.

"Thank you for taking care of him," she said a moment later, her gratitude encompassing both Abby and Joel as she took each of her children by the hand to lead them onto the path. "I have a big surprise," she was telling them as they walked away. "I saved some galettes from the ball especially for the two of you, and they're the kind you like best, the ones with blackberry perserves between the cookies."

The sounds of the children's enthusiastic responses faded as the trio walked on, and at the same time Abby's smile faded, too. Sitting on the bench, gazing thoughtfully at the ground, she nibbled at her upper lip, then looked at Joel when he sat down beside her.

"That cut was worse than I thought at first," she stated abruptly, worry written on her face. "Are you absolutely sure it was enough to just bandage it?"

"Who's the doctor here?" Joel replied with a teasing grin, taking one of her hands in both his. "Some antiseptic and a bandage were the only care the cut needed. It really wasn't that deep."

"But it bled more than it should have, didn't it?" she persisted, her fingers curving over the large hand beneath hers and tightly squeezing. "I'm not sure it really ever stopped bleeding. It still was when you took my handkerchief off it, and—"

"Abby, that marble corner is almost razor sharp and you know clean cuts bleed longer, even one like Davy's, which is really little more than a scratch. And the bandage

144

I put over it applies just enough pressure to keep it from bleeding. It had already stopped before Davy left with Faye."

"You're sure?" Abby believed what Joel said, yet lingering concern still shadowed her features as she looked at him. "You're absolutely sure Davy doesn't need a few stitches?"

"Stitches! Of course not." A perplexed frown furrowed Joel's brow as he gently grasped her upper arms. "Abby, Davy's arm was barely more than scratched, and I don't understand why you're so upset now that you're actually shaking. When Davy fell, you didn't panic, and when you were helping me with him, you were calm. But now . . . What's the matter with you?"

She was overreacting. That was what was the matter, she realized, as Joel's words sank in. Once in a rare while an incident as minor as that one would seem to literally propel her back to her childhood, to one of those times when her uncle Ted, a late baby and only five years her senior, had suffered a slight cut or bruise that was never a minor injury for him. Always then too, she had remained calm and comforting and helpful until the ambulance arrived to rush away, the siren screeching, toward the hospital with him. Only then had she gone to her room and trembled for hours in the throes of traumatic delayed reaction, as she was beginning to tremble now. But Davy was not Ted, and she couldn't allow herself to be overcome by fear without reason, and that simple self-analysis of what she was feeling and why enabled her to become calm immediately.

Tilting her chin up determinedly, she gave Joel a somewhat sheepish smile. "Of course I know you're right and that Davy's fine. Sometimes I just get unreasonably upset when a child is hurt."

"You certainly did an admirable job of hiding how upset you were from Davy."

145

"That's me. Cool and calm during a crisis and a total wreck when it's over," Abby said, laughing at herself, which was about all she could do in those circumstances. "That's the way I am."

"That simplistic statement can never describe what you are, Abby. You're much more complex than that," Joel contradicted, his dark eyes searching deeply into hers. "Actually, you're probably the most complicated person I've ever met."

"Is that why I am so irresistibly intriguing? *Oui, Docteur?*" she whispered her parody of a femme fatale, accompanied by a winsome smile. And when Joel couldn't help smiling back, she lifted her arms up and around his neck and brushed her lips across his, indomitably pushing thoughts of the past and Ted and the events of that afternoon far back in her mind.

Abby would never know what caused her to cry in her sleep that night. When she awakened to the sound of her own soft sobbing and Joel's low-timbred words of concern, she didn't feel she had been in the grip of a dream; she was simply crying. Her pillow was damp with fallen tears, tears that continued to flow even when she turned over in Joel's embrace and pressed her face against him. It was the strangest experience—crying without having any idea why. She suspected the tears might have come as a result of Davy's mishap that afternoon, but surely that would have induced an unforgettable nightmare. However, Abby remembered nothing between the time she had drifted peacefully off to sleep and the moment she had awakened crying. She didn't seem able to stop. Her nearly silent sobs were beyond her control and seemed to rise up from the very center of her being. She held Joel closer to her, needing his strength and his warmth.

Wisely Joel said nothing while simply massaging her back for several minutes until at last her tears were flowing

146

less profusely and fewer tremors were running through her slight body. Even then he didn't speak right away. Instead, he took several tissues from a decorator container on the bedside table and pressed them into her hand.

Feeling the light kiss he brushed across her hair, Abby blotted her cheeks, then touched tentative fingertips against his broad bare chest. "I got you all wet," she muttered, hiccuped, then laughed, though still rather tearfully. "I'm sorry, Joel."

"It's all right. Hush now, Abby. Try to relax," he coaxed softly, kissing her forehead, the damp fringe of her lashes, and the hollows of her cheeks. "Umm, still delicious but a bit too salty." His fingertips were now tracing the shape of her lips and he obviously felt them curve in a tremulous smile. "That's more like it. Feeling better?"

Nodding, she curled closer to him and did relax as the heat of his body penetrated her skin and warmed her, yet she was still confused. She so rarely cried that she could hardly believe she had awakened from a sound sleep in a veritable deluge of tears she had been totally unable to staunch. And she could imagine Joel must be feeling even more confused than she was, since she had never allowed herself to cry in front of him. Feeling she must say something to him, she whispered against his shoulder, "I'm sorry I woke you up, Joel."

"I'm not. I wouldn't have wanted you to cry in the darkness all alone," he whispered back, smoothing her hair. "But what was wrong, baby? A nightmare?"

Abby shook her head.

"Why were you crying, then?"

"That's the crazy thing about it—I have no idea why. Obviously, you knew I was crying before I did. I wasn't even awake until I heard you saying my name."

"But, Abby, that doesn't make sense. To wake up crying like that you must have been having an unhappy dream."

"If I was, I don't remember anything about it," she told him, and it was true. Not even fragments of a disturbing dream came to mind now, and she could only deduce that her subconscious had forced a release of tears she had too long consciously suppressed. And perhaps it was good. At that moment she did feel less tense than she had in several days, as if the spilling of tears had lightened her spirit. Once again she felt only that that moment in time mattered and she must find all the happiness she could in it, happiness she and Joel would share. She pressed harder against him, adoring the feel of his strong body against her bare skin. Her hand began to move in caressingly light circles over his chest and abdomen until he swiftly caught her fingers in his and she murmured a little protest.

"Don't start that just to avoid my question," he commanded quietly but firmly. "If you really don't remember dreaming, you must have been crying for some other reason."

"Not necessarily," she countered, moving until she was lying half across him, her warm breasts yielding to his harder flesh. "I'm a woman, and women cry sometimes. It's not unusual."

"For you it is. I've never seen you cry before."

"Well, now, you know I'm just like most other women; I do cry sometimes," she said in a silky whisper, kissing slowly, provocatively, the line of his strong jaw, from where it began beneath one ear around to the lobe of the other, which she tenderly nibbled.

"*Abby,* for God's sake. I'm trying to talk to you," Joel groaned, even as his arms tightened around her slender body. "Sometimes, like tonight, I have this feeling that something is actually tormenting you."

"Right now *you're* tormenting me. If you don't kiss me soon, I think I'll go crazy," she murmured, her lissome body moving invitingly against him. She leaned over him, gazing down at the barely perceptible contours of his chis-

148

eled face in the semidarkness. With one fingertip she traced the firmly outlined shape of his lips, smiling secretively to herself when she detected the increase of his breathing. She lowered her head, and golden tresses fell forward to brush his lean cheeks as she grazed her lips over first one corner of his mouth, then the other, again and again, pleased with the sure knowledge that this time her desire was arousing him.

Joel's response was as swift and impassioned as she could have wished. In one fluid motion he turned and arched her against him, the demanding pressure of his mouth taking possession of hers breathtaking in intensity. Abby returned his kisses, and tremors of delight flowed up and down her spine as the hardening of his lips was echoed throughout the length of his body.

They touched each other, explored each other, aroused each other's passion, to a fever pitch. Despite the white-hot intensity of Joel's desire, he was even more gentle with Abby than usual. His tenderly whispered endearments filled her with joy. His questing hands conveyed unparalleled sensitivity and roamed slowly over her, as if he were memorizing every exquisite detail of her delightfully curved body. His coaxing lips savored her kisses. He made her feel as if she were a fragile, priceless treasure safe in his keeping, and she had never loved him more than she did in that precious moment. As they were swept together closer and closer to that poignant, intimate realm only the two of them could share, Abby became lost in a spellbinding fantasy, a fantasy in which that night never ended, and she was forever with Joel, giving all her love to him.

CHAPTER TEN

It was compulsion that had brought Abby to Charleston and the medical center the next morning. It was always compulsion that brought her there. As she sat waiting in a small office, glancing around at the walls nearly completely covered with diplomas from several prestigious medical schools and various certificates to practice, the tiny bud of hope she had awakened with that morning neither blossomed nor died. It was simply there and had come from nowhere as it did on occasion. Wondering if she would ever possess the willpower to resist succumbing to even that minute hope, she stared out the window over the rooftops of surrounding buildings, so lost in thought, she didn't even hear the office door being opened quietly.

What gained her attention were the huge hands laid lightly on her shoulders and the gruff voice from behind her saying, "Nurse Wilcox told me you were here. Abby, are you absolutely sure you want to go through this again?"

She nodded. "I'm sure. You know I'm plagued by a need to come have the tests done at least once a year. As long as I feel there's even the slimmest possibility the results might be different just one time, I have to come here. I guess it's silly, but—"

"No, not silly, Abby. Perfectly natural, I think," David Howard assured her, patting a shoulder comfortingly when she tilted her head back to look up at him. "I understand how you must feel and I want you to know that whenever that need to be retested comes over you, I'll send you right down to the lab."

"Even though you think it's absolutely useless to go through the whole procedure again," she questioned almost inaudibly. "Is that what you really want to say?"

"No, I'd never say that, actually. Since I've been practicing medicine I've seen at least one patient recover from a condition some of the finest physicians in the country had diagnosed as hopeless and I've heard about others so, no, I won't tell you it's useless to have these tests done again." Frowning thoughtfully, David walked around Abby's chair to sit down behind a desk that was nearly dwarfed by the impressive size of his frame. Propping his elbows on the ink blotter, he cupped his chin in his hands and looked directly into her eyes. "And there's absolutely no harm in your having the tests once in a while . . . as long as you remember that the possibility of the results changing is very remote."

"That's something I can really never forget," Abby murmured. "But always, in the back of my mind, I remember that sometimes the tests can show false positives."

"True." David nodded, and compassion was obvious on his broad honest face. "But you also know that the testing procedure is eighty to ninety percent accurate, and, Abby, every time you've had the tests done, the results have been positive."

"About time they changed, then, don't you think?" she responded with forced cheeriness. "And maybe this will be my lucky day."

"Maybe."

"But you seriously doubt it?"

"Yes, I'm sorry to have to say that I do doubt it very much. And I hate to see you getting your hopes up this way."

"Don't worry, David," she said, her expression somber again. "I know better than to let my hopes get too high, and as soon as I begin to feel any at all, I hurry right over here to be retested. If the results are going to be positive, it's better to still these unreasonable little stirrings of hope I have occasionally right away, before they have a chance to grow too strong."

"I see. The greater the hope, the more severe the disappointment would be." When Abby nodded, David's professional demeanor dropped away and the sentiments his eyes expressed were those of a personal friend. Smiling at her with respectful fondness, he leaned forward, his arms resting atop the desk. "You're one of my favorite people, Abby. Did you know that?"

"I hoped I might be, because you're certainly one of my favorite people," she answered sincerely, brushing a crescent of flaxen hair back from her temple. "You don't treat me like a patient; you treat me like a friend, and it's so good to know I can talk to you about *everything*."

Understanding exactly what she meant, David regarded her intently. "But surely there are people at the Hemophilia Foundation you can talk freely with?"

"I've never told anyone there that I'm a carrier," she responded emphatically. "It's not something I've ever talked about a lot—I'd hate to start dwelling on it. And now I don't dare tell anyone in Charleston, for fear it might somehow get back to—"

"Joel," he finished for her when she hesitated. Concern tightened his rugged features and he sighed heavily. "Abby, I realize how difficult the past week and a half has been for you. Faye . . . well, she mentioned trying to bring

152

you and Joel back together again, but I knew how distressed you'd be if she went through with her well-meaning little plot. Frankly, I thought I talked her out of playing matchmaker and was probably almost as surprised as you and Joel were when it turned out she had invited the two of you to spend two weeks at Fairfields at the same time. Of course I knew Joel was coming but I didn't know about you. When Faye is certain she's doing the right thing, she can be something of a sneak. I only hope the past days haven't been too terribly nerve-racking for you."

"I've probably never spent a more nerve-racking time in my life," she admitted, then qualified her response and smiled wistfully. "But, oddly enough, I've felt happy too, much happier than I've been the last four months."

"You're obviously still very much in love with Joel."

"How could you tell?" Abby asked pertly, something of sadness even in her mischievous smile. "And I thought I was hiding it so well."

"You are probably hiding it pretty well. But don't forget, I'm the only person who knows you loved him so much, you felt you had to end everything with him a few months back. And, knowing the kind of woman you are, it only makes sense for me to believe you still love him, or the two of you wouldn't have been so close, actually sharing a bedroom, since the night of the ball. Abby, since you've gotten back with him at Fairfields, don't you think the relationship could work out right this time?"

"I wish," she mumbled, but shook her head. "Our relationship now is just a temporary one. I knew that when I let it begin but, believe it or not, I gambled and decided to take as much happiness as I could *while* I could, and I hope I won't live to regret it."

"I think you're making a mistake," David stated bluntly. "You should tell Joel the truth about yourself."

"I can't, especially now. Whatever Joel felt for me four

months ago was killed when I ended our relationship. About all he feels for me these days is a physical attraction, and if I were to tell him I'm a hemophilia carrier, he'd run for the hills. I've had to accept that," Abby said. Then the shadow of sadness in her aqua eyes swiftly vanished to be replaced by a resolute gleam. She moved forward in her chair. "But you know what, David? If I could just get a negative result on these tests one time, I'd do everything in my power to win Joel's love, because then there'd be a chance I could give him the children he wants so much."

David's expression was pained. "It isn't wise of you to stake your entire future on test results," he counseled gently. "I hate to know that's what you're doing."

"I don't have any other choice."

"But, Abby, the odds against the results being negative are astronomically high. And you know that, so why be so stubborn? Tell Joel the truth and see what happens."

"I can't. I won't, and don't you see why?" Abby exclaimed softly. "If I told him the truth, and if the mere word *hemophilia* horrified him so much he couldn't hide his reaction, I think I'd want to die. And I don't want to have to deal with that kind of pain or to have to try to erase the memory of his reaction. I want to make my life as happy as I possibly can, and such a devastating memory would just make that more difficult."

"But Abby, you—"

"No, David," she reiterated firmly, lifting one hand to halt his words. "Let's talk about something else."

David sighed but also nodded. "All right. What would you like to talk about? Any news you haven't told me?"

"As a matter of fact, yes." Abby smiled at his resigned expression. "My sister is pregnant and very excited about it."

"That must cause you some pain," David suggested as he tapped the eraser end of a pencil on the ink blotter. "It must seem unfair to you that your older sister can have children without any fear but you can't."

"I'm very happy for Sue," Abby replied calmly, and meant it. "And my mother has reminded me many times that since I can't have a family, I can devote myself to my career. She's right, and I don't think of it as unfair that Sue can have children."

"Abby . . ."

"All right, it hurts a little, but I've never resented Sue because of my situation. And if I could snap my fingers this very moment and make her the carrier instead of me, I wouldn't do that to her. I only wish that we both could have been born lucky, but the odds were against me. It's as simple as that."

"'As simple as that,'" David repeated, shaking his head. "Honey, you amaze me sometimes. I *know* how this lousy defective gene has complicated your life, but you try to shrug it off and call it simple. Abby, you don't have to be so brave all the time."

"Brave? Me?" Abby's short laugh was edged by huskiness. "Oh, if you only knew how often I feel like running and hiding."

"You never show those feelings outwardly."

"I've always tried not to, but these days I'm not having much success at it. Joel thinks I'm the moodiest person he's ever known. Actually, I suspect he thinks I'm a borderline neurotic."

"But if Joel knew the truth—"

"I have to go and let you get back to your patients," Abby cut in, unwilling to backtrack to that particular topic. Besides, she was revealing too many of her inner feelings to David, and revealing them made them more difficult to suppress. She needed to talk to him, but only up to a point, and that point had already been passed that day. Rising from her chair, she smiled graciously at him. "Anyway, I need to get back to Fairfields quickly. I told

155

Faye and Joel that the office needed me to attend to an urgent matter but that it wouldn't take long. If I'm not back soon, Joel might call the agency. And, David, I hope you know how grateful I am that you let me just barge in here sometimes, without an appointment."

"You never barge in, Abby. And I want you to come see me any time you need to, even if it's only to talk," David said sincerely, tearing a sheet off a prescription pad, then scribbling something across the back. He stood and came around the desk to hand the sheet to her. "Order for the tests. Give it to Tom in the lab. I've instructed him to get the results to me 'stat.' "

"That's medical jargon for pretty damn quick, isn't it? See, I did learn something during my stint as a volunteer in pediatrics," Abby said with a half smile that blossomed to a full one when she looked up at David. "Thanks for asking for the results as soon as possible. It sure is nice to have influential friends." As she stretched up on tiptoe to kiss his cheek her tone became more serious. "And you're a very dear friend, too. I know Faye must tell you she's sure something's bothering me, and you can't tell her exactly what the problem is. I wouldn't mind her knowing about the hemophilia, except . . . well, I think if she knew, she'd tell Joel because she would really believe it might help our relationship, which, of course, it wouldn't."

"I'm not at all sure you're right about that, Abby," David said softly. "I think maybe Joel should know."

"Bye, David. See you this evening" was Abby's evasive response. After waving back over her shoulder to him, she left his office to go down to the lab, which she felt she could have found blindfolded.

Ominous and rolling gray-black clouds were gathering in the sky over Fairfields early in the evening before twilight. Gusts of wind chased a few fallen magnolia leaves over the wide expanse of lawn and bent the tops of sur-

156

rounding trees that sprang up straight again after each gust subsided and before another swooshed over them. Despite the fact that the storm clouds were directly overhead, the rumbling thunder was still distant and there had been no close flashes of lightning as yet.

In the living room, where Abby and Joel had joined Faye and the children, it was as if the increasingly electric-charged air outside engendered more activity in the house. Ellie and Davy chattered incessantly as they played on the floor with a toy village inhabited by families of round, fairly undetailed little dolls that they called "poopies." While they engaged in animated make-believe Faye wandered around the room, straightening a figurine here, rearranging flowers in a vase there. Only Abby and Joel seemed able to sit quietly on the sofa together, and even then the coming storm had brought a subtle glow of excitement to Abby's aqua eyes.

"I remember that look," Joel murmured so only she could hear. "You like storms."

"Especially when I'm safe inside," she admitted, smiling lazily at him. "I feel very secure somehow."

"And inclined to cuddle, I remember," he said, a half-teasing, half-provocative glimmer in his dark eyes as his gaze wandered over the pretty picture she made in an ice-blue dress with her shimmering hair softly framing her face. His arm was draped across her shoulders and his fingertips began to draw small caressing circles on her bare upper arm as he added, "You certainly look almost irresistibly cuddly now."

"Resist. We'll cuddle later," she promised, reaching out to unnecessarily adjust the open collar of his white shirt beneath his blazer, allowing her fingers to linger on the smooth sun-browned skin of his neck. "But I have to admit you look very cuddly, too."

Acting for all the world like two newlyweds completely absorbed in each other, they exchanged a light kiss, then reluctantly turned their attention to the playing children again.

Across the room, Faye sighed abruptly while standing at the closed French doors, gazing out at the windswept garden. After a few seconds, she glanced at her wristwatch. "David should be home any minute now. Probably before the storm breaks . . . unless he's late."

"He said it was Peterson's night to do hospital rounds, didn't he?" Joel asked, and when Faye nodded, he gave her a reassuring smile. "I doubt he'll be late, then. It isn't often doctors get to leave the office at the end of office hours, so we make certain we never miss an opportunity."

Faye smiled sheepishly. "I know you're right. I just get a little uneasy when everyone's not safe in the house during a storm."

Joel's words soon proved prophetic. Less than two minutes later the front door was opened, and David's hearty greeting boomed and echoed in the main hall. Abby smiled understandingly at Faye when she heaved a great sigh of relief, then went to meet her husband as he entered the living room. Ellie and Davy weren't far behind, and after their parents kissed, both children clamored to be the first David swooped up and swung around once in the air. It was a daily treat, almost a sacred tradition, and in a few moments both brother and sister were again safely on the ground, giggling and a trifle dizzy from the exciting ride.

With David home Faye was able to settle peacefully in a chair while he proceeded across the room. "Bar's open. I assume you'll all have your regular," he said, then added casually, "Abby, honey, how about a little assist? Come fill the glasses with ice for me."

With a sharp little catch in her chest, Abby got up and went to the bar, knowing precisely why David had asked her to help him. He knew the results of her tests, the tests she had refused even to think about since she had left the lab. Now the results were in, and she had no choice except to think, but amazingly enough, the vague little hope she felt didn't suddenly bloom to full flower even then. Without being consciously aware of it she held tight rein over her emotions as she joined David behind the bar. There was silence between them as she filled two glasses with ice from a silver bucket.

"Well?" she finally prompted while dropping a cube in a third. "What's the verdict?"

"Positive. Again. Damn it, Abby, I'm sorry," David muttered, a muscle working furiously in his jaw. "Very sorry."

Hardly surprised the results were the same as they had always been, Abby inclined her head in a brief nod and gave her friend a small grateful smile. "Thank you for getting me the results so soon, David."

"You all right?" he questioned as she continued calmly to fill glasses with ice. "Abby?"

"I'm fine."

Sometimes it is more difficult to be the bearer of bad news than the recipient. Realizing that, Abby lightly and briefly touched David's sleeve to comfort him. "It's all right. Really," she told him softly, "it's not as if I had actually believed the results would be different this time."

And after bringing forth a tray for David to carry the drinks on when he finished mixing them, she went back to Joel, her expression so composed, no one could have possibly imagined she had just heard the last thing in the world she wanted to hear. Already she had pushed David's news far back into a small dark room in her mind, then closed and locked a door on it, a defense mechanism her situation and time had taught her to be quite adept at utilizing.

The evening passed pleasantly as all evenings at Fairfields seemed to. Abby enjoyed playing with and talking to the children until their bedtime arrived, then equally enjoyed a relaxing conversation with Faye, Joel, and David. Yet, when the elder Howards retired soon after eleven o'clock, she certainly wasn't sorry to have Joel to herself again.

Together they went upstairs to their room and closed the door behind them but, for a moment, didn't switch on the lights. They stood silently, looking out the French doors that opened onto the balcony and watching sheet lightning glow at brief intervals in the cloud-banked night sky. Occasionally a more dramatic jagged lightning bolt split the clouds and bathed the bedroom in soft illumination for an instant while sharp claps of thunder followed close behind. The storm of early evening had been the first in a front that was slowly traveling along the South Carolina coastline and, all in all, it had been a turbulent night. With the unbidden thought of how frightening it would be to be out on a boat in the ocean during the storm, which so far was the most severe of the evening, Abby shivered, then relaxed against Joel's side as his arm around her waist tightened. Her soft cheek brushed the fabric of his blazer, and she closed her eyes.

"Mmm, it's nice not to have to be out in that, isn't it?" she said softly, putting her arms around him. "And it's the perfect night for cuddling, don't you agree, Doctor?"

"I couldn't agree more, but before we become very heavily involved in that, there's something else I want to do," Joel told her, a hint of mystery edging his low tone of voice. Releasing her, he went to switch on the bedside lamp, then walked to the huge walk-in closet to open the louvered doors. After removing a rectangular parcel wrapped in plain brown paper, he brought it to Abby, who took it with a puzzled, but decidedly delighted, expression highlighting her delicate features.

"For me? But what is it?"

"Open it and see," he instructed. Taking her by the hand, he led her to the bed, where she sat on the edge while he stood leaning against one of the four tall posts and looking down at her. "Well, aren't you going to open it?"

Smiling excitedly, Abby carefully lifted the tape securing one pleated corner of the paper, then the other three, and finally opened the parcel. What she discovered was the back of a wooden-framed canvas. "Oh, a painting!" A sudden thought struck her and her eyes darted up to Joel's face, then back down. "It isn't? It is!" she murmured, turning the frame around and finding the J. Earl painting of the secluded cove that Joel had purchased at the gallery. Simply looking at it evoked beautiful memories of her night with Joel on the *Sea Nymph,* and she could only hope there wasn't a revealing glistening of moisture in her eyes when she looked back up at him.

"Oh, Joel. But *you* wanted this painting," she protested softly. "You don't have to give it to me."

"I don't have to do anything. I want you to have it because you did say it was your favorite, didn't you?

"Well, yes, but—"

"Tell me why. Why was that particular painting your favorite, Abby?" Joel asked, moving with lithe swiftness to sit beside her on the bed's edge. His enigmatic gaze captured and held hers. "Could it be that the cove reminds you of the one where we anchored the *Sea Nymph?*"

"Yes," she said almost inaudibly, unable to lie because of the strangely compelling glow in his dark eyes. "It is very much like the cove where we anchored. But—" Her words faltered as disappointment swept through her because he was so willingly giving the painting to her. It must not have meant much to him that it so resembled their cove. Yet it was unreasonable to *expect* it to mean anything to him, and she tried to ignore her disappointment. She took a long deep breath, still looking at him. "You don't want the painting, then?"

"Oh, I didn't exactly say that, Abby," he whispered inscrutably, removing the frame from her hands and lying

161

the canvas on the chest at the foot of the bed. "No, I didn't say that at all."

"Joel, I don't understand," she murmured, then understood even less when his large hands possessively spanned her waist and his intense dark eyes seemed to burn through her. "Joel?"

The instant she tentatively laid her hand against his cheek, he pulled her into his arms and whispered urgently, "*Abby*. God, I love you," before his warm lips parted hers in a passionately adoring kiss.

Joy surged up in Abby. The unexpected words, yet words she had secretly ached to hear, became the only reality and filled her with happiness to the very core of her being. She pressed closer to Joel and, as the minty freshness of his mouth, his warmth, and his gentle strength made her senses reel, her own words tumbled out. "Oh, I love you too, Joel. So much. So much," she breathed between their deepening kisses. "I love you more than anything."

"Thank God you do," he said huskily, his lips blazing a fiery trail along her slender neck. "Now we can stop this foolish nonsense of pretending this is no more than what you called 'a sex holiday' and get married right away. The sooner the better, don't you think?"

Abby was suddenly very still, then began to shake violently. All strength drained from her limbs as Joel's words reverberated in her brain, destroying her ability to think clearly. It was all she could do to pull away from Joel slightly and stare up at him, her eyes haunted as she uttered hoarsely, "Married?"

"Of course. We have to get married now, don't we, Abby?" He wound a wayward strand of silken hair around one of his long fingers. "How else can we both have the painting of the cove?"

The endearing smile that lightly crinkled his tan face and lighted his dark eyes seemed to wrench Abby's very

162

soul from her body. Two opposing forces were tearing her to pieces, one of them saying "Marry him! Marry him now and tell the truth later" while the other screamed "You can't do that to him. You *can't* !" The force urging self-sacrifice proved stronger and won the battle raging inside her. Slight nausea stirred in her stomach as she felt as if the earth had suddenly dropped from beneath her feet and left her plummeting forever into a vast emptiness. Her entire body burned before going clammy cold when the full realization of what she had done exploded in her mind. She stared at Joel, her chest raw with the pain of love that couldn't be completely given. She had convinced herself to take as much happiness as she could for as long as possible because Joel's interest in her was strictly physical, and he would be able to walk away from their relationship unscathed when it ended. But she had been wrong, so very wrong. Now his feelings were involved, and she was consumed by a horrid guilt at what she had done. She would have to end everything between them again, just as she had four months earlier, and she wouldn't be able to tell him the reason she had to leave him this time either.

A tortured groan rose in her throat, and she bit down hard on her lower lip to hold it in as she looked at the man she loved, the man who would want children she couldn't give him. Yet, despite that, she knew in that moment that she would do anything to keep him with her, anything at all . . . except marry him.

CHAPTER ELEVEN

As if she had been deprived of oxygen for an eternity of time, Abby took a long gulping breath. There was something of an entreaty in her ragged voice when she said, "But . . . Joel, you aren't serious about . . . marriage. You . . . said 'no strings attached.' "

"I lied," he retorted blithely, but shook his head as his right hand curved around her neck to caress her nape. "Not really. I meant it when I said no strings attached. I thought it could be that way, but it didn't quite work out like that. I loved you four months ago and I love you even more now. I guess I never stopped caring, though I tried my damnedest."

Unshed tears gathered to create an agonizing pressure behind Abby's eyes, and she lowered her head, her voice scratchy and greatly strained as she uttered, "Oh, Joel, please . . ."

" 'Oh, Joel, please' what?" he questioned gently, raising her small chin with one finger. His searching gaze played over her unusually pale face. "Abby, what's wrong? You just said you love me, too. That's true, isn't it?"

"Yes, oh, yes. I love you," she whispered. That she

couldn't force herself to lie about. "But marriage, Joel
. . . I'm not sure we should really even consider that."

His dark brows lifted questioningly but he smiled still.
"Why shouldn't we consider getting married? Most people in love eventually do."

Abby started to touch him, knew she shouldn't, and
dropped her hands into her lap to clench them tightly
together. She spoke a word, faltered, began again. "I guess
I just think we're not like most other people. I mean,
should we really get married when we're both so heavily
involved in our careers?"

"I can't see what that has to do with it, frankly. I know
many people who are happily married although they both
have careers."

"But your career is so demanding, and in many ways
mine is, too. If we married, our work might somehow put
a . . . strain on our relationship."

A faint frown broke on Joel's forehead. "Abby, that
doesn't make any sense whatsoever."

Desperation took hold of her and she leaned toward
him, catching his face between her hands. "But I don't see
why we have to get married. What's wrong with the way
things are now? Can't we go on just like this? You asked
me to live with you four months ago. Well, now I can say
yes. I want very much to live with you."

"But I want a permanent relationship now, Abby. Simply living with you wouldn't be enough for me," he told
her, his hands moving on her shoulders, massaging coaxingly. "At my age I'm ready for the responsibility of a
family. I want you to be my wife, the mo—"

"Just for a little while, let's keep it the way it is now,"
she blurted out, cutting him short before he could finish
saying those most devastating of words: *the mother of my
children.* She couldn't have withstood the pain of hearing
him say that. With her nerves frayed immeasurably already, a sudden bright streak of lightning, followed by a

165

deafening crack of thunder, threatened to shatter her tortured emotions into too many fragments for them ever to be really mended. Realizing that only a fragile thread of sheer willpower was preventing her from bursting into tears, she strove to gather what remained of her resources of inner strength. Unfortunately, those resources were very nearly depleted, and she found she could no longer control her trembling. Her fingers shook against his lean cheeks as she whispered beseechingly, "Joel, we could be happy living together. I know it."

"That wouldn't be enough for me now," he said, a building irritation edging his voice. "I lost you once, Abby, but I won't risk that again. I won't be satisfied with anything less than marriage. You're going to have to marry me, and that's that."

That's that. How right he was. That was it. And realizing how hopeless it all had come to be, Abby made a low sorrowful sound. Pain shafted through her, the pain of love lost yet again so severe that she was paralyzed in the grip of it. Then the pain subsided, and she was filled with something even worse—relentless emptiness. She felt hollow, empty of everything except the knowledge that this was the end. She had to make the break with Joel fast and final and she had to make it then. Her hands dropped limply from his face.

"I can't," she mumbled, unable to bear looking at him. "I can't . . . marry you."

"The hell you can't! Just say yes," he commanded impatiently. "Abby, I don't want to hear any more of your nonsense about us both being too involved in our careers."

"It isn't . . . only that."

"Then what else is there?" he muttered harshly, his hold on her shoulders becoming a viselike grip. Anger flared up in him, and heightened color suffused his cheeks beneath his tan as he shook her once. "I asked you what else there could be. Is it another man? Someone in

166

Charleston? You've gone back there alone twice since we've been here. To see him?"

"No, Joel! There's no one else. There's never been any man more important to me than you, but . . ." She pressed her fingers against her aching eyes as she finished, ". . . I can't marry you. I *can't.*"

"Damn it, Abby, why can't you?" he asked, his voice less harsh now, his tone more gently probing. His long fingers encircled her delicately boned wrists and he drew her hands from her face. "Give me one good reason why you can't marry me."

She could have given him the perfect reason—the truth. But secrets too long kept locked deep in the heart are not so easily revealed, and Abby's fear of Joel's rejection would not allow her to tell him the complete truth, only a half-truth, which can be on occasion worse than a lie. She stared down at his hands, which still held her wrists, and tried to banish all remaining emotion in order to be able to give a convincing performance. When at last she looked up to face Joel directly again, her features were remarkably composed, as a result of another of those self-protective tricks she had learned over the years.

"I think I do have a good reason to say I can't marry you," she stated tonelessly, seeming to look right into his brown eyes while willing herself not to really see them. "If we did marry, Joel, it wouldn't work out. There are irreconcilable differences between us."

His confusion was obvious and he appeared to be quickly losing patience again. "I may be dense but I'm not aware of any irreconcilable differences. Maybe you'd better name one of them."

Abby's throat felt parched and she swallowed convulsively as she gestured vaguely with one hand. "All right. You . . . want to have children. Don't you, Joel?"

"Well, sure, but what's that got to do with any of this nonsense. Abby—"

"I don't. I don't want to have children," she lied, and realized with the sudden agonizing constriction in her chest that she hadn't managed to banish all her feelings. She began to tremble all over once again. "Wouldn't you call that an irreconcilable difference?"

"For God's sake, I don't expect you to be thinking about having children already," he said, more than a little exasperated. "We won't be thinking of that for some time. We're just talking about getting married now."

"You don't seem to understand," she murmured, unable to control the quavering of her voice. "I won't ever want to think about having children, because I never want any. Ever. They . . . just don't fit into my plans for the future. My career—"

"Many women have both children and careers."

Abby couldn't bear much more of it. The lie she was being forced to utter again and again was such a blatant untruth, the antithesis of her real feelings, and she couldn't go on lying much longer. She had to end it then. She pulled her hands resolutely from Joel's and hugged her arms across her breasts.

"I'm not other women. I actually have no desire for children; they . . . make me uncomfortable and they're disruptive," she told him, her eyes riveted on the tan column of his neck rising above his open collar. "For me, babies and a career wouldn't mix. My responsibilities at home would keep me from advancing as rapidly in the agency."

"It wouldn't necessarily have to be that way," Joel said, more perplexed than exasperated now. He carefully surveyed her face. His voice deepened as his tone conveyed an intensifying solemnity. "I'm sure we can come to some agreement on this if we're willing to be reasonable and talk it out."

"But there's nothing to talk about," Abby mumbled, staring at Joel's feet, the acute pain in her chest sharpening

168

with every passing second. "I doubt you'd ever be willing *not* to have children, and I'd never be willing *to* have any."

Joel stiffened beside her and his hand was less than gentle when he gripped her chin and tilted her head back so she had to face him. "Are you actually refusing even to discuss this with me?" When she gave no answer at all, which was an answer in itself, he breathed an explicit oath, his deep voice cold, hard, and devoid of respect. "You're right, then. We do have irreconcilable differences."

"Oh, but I do love you!" Abby whispered frantically before she could prevent herself, reaching out to curve her hand over his shoulders before he could stand up. "I love you more than—"

"I find that very difficult to believe," he cut in icily, his face a hard mask. As if he could scarcely bear her touch, he removed her hands from his shoulders and put them away from him, then rose to his feet to tower over her. His jaw hardened; his lips compressed disdainfully as he stared down at her. "I don't want any part of *your* kind of love, Abby. And I think you should know that it isn't the fact that you don't want children and I do that's our real irreconcilable difference. Our problem is your unwillingness to communicate with me, even to talk to me about something like this. I'm damn tired of your secretiveness. I'm going downstairs to make myself a drink, and when I come back, either you can sleep in your room or I will. Understood?"

As he thrust his hands deep in his pocket, turned, and started to walk away, a crushing sense of loss descended on Abby. Tears welled in her eyes, and Joel was a blurred form as he approached the door to the hallway. Yet, even with sight distorted, she detected the uncharacteristic heaviness in the very way he moved. There was a piercing catch in her heart as she suddenly realized how unfair she was being. She had thought she would never be able to bear Joel's rejection but now knew that even that pain would be preferable to allowing him to believe she was rejecting him. If he loved her at all, or even only believed that he did, he was hurting, and she couldn't stand that. She owed him the truth, or at least enough of it to make him understand that it was her own lack, not his, that wouldn't allow her to marry him. At that moment her own pain mattered much less to her than his, and she couldn't let him go like that, thinking what he did.

Emitting a strangled little cry, she propelled herself off the bed and ran after him, reaching him as his hand grasped the door handle. "Joel, wait!" she exclaimed softly, hesitantly touching his broad back. "I—lied to you."

"You're damn right you did. I just realized it," he muttered, startling her with his furious vehemence and the roughness of the hand that grasped her upper arm when he turned away from the door. His dark eyes were hostile, his expression grim, as he impelled her across the room to the cedarwood tapestry-upholstered divan, where she sank down on the edge, her entire body trembling. When she started to speak, he interrupted tersely, "Don't try telling me again that you can't marry me because I want children and they make you uncomfortable. I know that's a lie. I've seen you too often with Davy and Ellie and you care about them. And Valerie's baby—you could hardly keep your hands off him. And you certainly wouldn't have done volunteer work in pediatrics if kids made you ill at ease. I'm not stupid, Abby; the question of children has nothing to do with us. There is another man, isn't there?"

"No. No, there isn't anyone else. I—"

"Damn it, Abby, you'd better tell me the truth."

"Yes. The truth," she murmured bleakly, realizing she was facing the most heartrending moment of her life as she forced herself to raise her head and look up at the hardened, unrelenting contours of his lean face. His anger was almost tangible, and her soul's secret, so long kept, tried to bury itself deeper, but with phenomonal strength of will she dragged it forth while clenching her hands together so tightly that her nails dug into her palms. "There is no other man, Joel, but—you're right about my feelings for children. They don't make me uncomfortable at all—actually, I—adore them," she began falteringly, then forced the next words out in a rush. "And it's not that I wouldn't want to have your children. The truth I haven't been able to tell you is that I *can't* have any. I *can't* have children."

"Don't insult me with another lie! Do you think I'm some kind of fool?" Joel ground out, taking one menacing step closer to her. "Considering the precautions you insist on taking to prevent a pregnancy, how the hell am I supposed to believe now that you *can't* have a baby?"

"All right, I could get pregnant. I could have a baby. But I can't ever let that happen." *Tell him the whole truth; get it over with,* the more pragmatic side of her was nagging, yet the complete truth stuck in her throat, and she could only elude to it. "I really can't have children, Joel, but not because I'm physically incapable of having them."

"If the reason isn't physical, then what is it? Emotional?" he persisted, his expression dubious, as if he were unable to believe a word she had said. "Does the thought of being pregnant scare you, or are you afraid of having to go through labor and delivery?"

She could have easily released a torrent of tears then but didn't, fearing she might never stop crying once she began. Instead, she sadly shook her head. "Joel, I'd gladly go through nine months of carrying your child inside me. And, although I'm sure it's no picnic, I'd even be happy to endure the labor and delivery, but I *can't*." After taking a deep shuddering breath, she made herself continue. "And the problem isn't emotional or actually physical. It's genetic. I wouldn't be doing a child a favor by having him, or her, for that matter."

"I think you'd better be specific, Abby," Joel said curtly, "because I'm having a great deal of trouble believing any of this, considering the lie you told me not five minutes ago. Exactly what do you mean when you say it's genetic?"

"Oh, God, you're going to make me say it, aren't you? You're going to make me say it all," she whispered desolately, looking down because she could no longer look at him. The strangling constriction in her throat made swallowing difficult and roughened her voice as she at last told him what she had never intended to tell. "It's—hemophilia. Mother's younger brother, Ted, is a hemophiliac. Mother is a carrier, and—" She heard Joel's anticipatory intake of breath but said the words anyhow. "And I'm a carrier, too."

The silence that followed became more than Abby could bear. She glanced up and saw the stunned expression on Joel's face and felt dead inside. Her tears had long since subsided. Sometimes life inflicts wounds that are too deep to be eased in the least by crying. Tears would come much later, Abby knew, but was able to feel only a modicum of relief that Joel would be nowhere around to witness them, too. Other than that, she felt almost numb. It was mainly a primitive need to go off somewhere alone to nurse her wounds that brought her to her feet.

"I'm going to pack now and drive back to Charleston. I need to be by myself," she droned on as she stared dully across the room. "Explain to Faye why I left. It doesn't matter if she knows the truth now, since you already do."

It was as if the first step she took toward the closet released Joel from his mild state of shock. One hand shot out to catch hold of hers, and he turned her around to face him. "Hemophilia," he repeated, utter astonishment obvious in his eyes, his face, his tone. He held both her hands now, tightly in his, as he shook his head slowly back and forth. "Abby, are you sure you're a carrier? Have you had the complete series of tests: the Factor Eight blood level,

172

coagulation activity, and antigen level, all of them? If you haven't—"

"Joel, I've had the entire series of tests more times than I want to remember," Abby said dully, her grim smile a parody. "What's really ironic is that I've just gone through all the tests again. And the very day David tells me the results are, of course, positive as always, you propose marriage. Don't you think that's the most ironic thing you've ever heard?"

"Abby . . ."

"Well, you know everything now," she continued flatly as if he hadn't spoken. She tugged wearily at her hands in a lackluster attempt to free herself of his grip, devoid of the energy it would have taken to make him release her. She could only look up at him, totally unaware of the rather defeated and lost expression shadowing the blue depths of her eyes. "I really want to be alone now, to go back to Charleston, so if you'd just let me go, I—"

"Oh, no, I'm not letting you go, not when I'm just beginning to understand so many things," Joel murmured, drawing her gently, but inexorably, over to the divan again, where he made her sit, then took his seat beside Abby, her small hand still firmly clasped between his. His eyes seemed to try to plumb the depths of hers until she bent her head, unable to continue meeting his too-knowing gaze. He mumbled something so softly, the words were incomprehensible but his touch became even more gentle as he said, "Of course, it all makes more sense now—your changeable moods, your crying in your sleep, your anxiety when Davy cut himself. Even— Damn, Abby, is this the reason you ended our relationship four months ago?"

When she nodded, and he uttered a muffled imprecation, she shrugged and asked, "What else could I do?"

"You could have told me the truth!" he exclaimed softly, emphatically, his hands moving to her waist, turning her back toward him. A series of emotions flitted over his carved features, too quickly to be identified. All that was recognizable was bewilderment. "For heaven's sake, Abby, why *didn't* you tell me about the hemophilia?"

"I couldn't. I just couldn't," she said, the word coming from between his lips almost causing her to flinch, despite the emptiness she felt. "Only my family and the doctors I've seen know about—this. It's not something I've been eager to tell anyone else."

"I'm not just anyone, Abby."

"No, you're much more important than anyone else! Don't you see? That's *why* you were the last person I thought I could tell, because—because I realized how much you wanted a son someday. . . ."

"Oh, my God," he muttered, briefly closing his eyes as his lips twisted in self-derision. "That time in my office, after the Dorsetts left with their baby, I asked how you'd like it if we had a child. And just the other day when we stayed with Valerie's baby, I told you you'd make a terrific mother someday. No wonder you ran up to your room, considering what you apparently believe to be true. If I'd only known that then—"

"Considering what I apparently believe to be true? What do you mean by that?"

"We'll discuss that in a minute. First I want you to tell me exactly how you feel," Joel commanded gently, getting up to bend over her, lifting her feet up onto the divan despite her weary attempt at resistance.

"Joel, what—"

"Talk to me, Abby," he coaxed, sitting back down beside her. "Tell me everything you feel about—"

"I don't want to lie on a couch and be—pyschoanalyzed," Abby protested, her voice breaking revealingly as, from her semireclining position on the divan, she struggled to sit up straight. The pressure of Joel's hand against her shoulder held her prisoner, and because overwrought emotions had taken a heavy toll on physical energy, she sank back down with an inward agonized moan. Why couldn't he just let her go? She needed so badly to be alone then and wasn't sure she could stand to lie there and be subjected to his inquisition. Yet it was obvious he intended to get answers to his questions, and she would only prolong the agony if she fought him. Turning her face aside on a small pillow, she muttered, "What is it you want to know? Tell you everything I feel about what?"

"About hemophilia," he replied quietly, stroking the back of her right hand as if to relax her. "About being a carrier. Tell me your true feelings."

An abbreviated laugh that sounded more like a bitter half sob escaped her lips. "I feel defective," she said aloud for the first time ever. "And why shouldn't I? That's precisely what I am. No matter how often my mother tells me I may not be able to have children but I can sure make a great success of my career, it doesn't compensate."

"She actually tells you you can't have children?"

Joel's abruptly sharp tone caused Abby to look up and see the stormy shadows in his eyes and the swift frown that furrowed his smooth brow. She shook her head. "Mother doesn't have to tell me something I know already. She simply tries to comfort me by encouraging me in my career."

"But—"

"She and my father gambled when they decided to have a baby, and when my older sister, Sue, was born, they were so relieved she was a girl, they never planned to press their luck again. But accidents happen, and I was one. And from what Mother's told me, that pregnancy was one long, hellish nightmare because she was afraid the odds were against her. She was terrified I'd be a boy and afflicted like Ted. He was just over five then, and she'd seen what he'd already had to go through. She so desperately wanted me to be a girl that she really couldn't worry that

175

I might be a carrier. When we learned I am . . . I think she was more upset than I was . . . at first."

"And your sister, Sue?" Joel probed gently. "She's not a carrier, I assume."

"No, she got lucky. She's pregnant now. And, yes, before you ask, I admit it does hurt me a little to know she can have children, and I—"

"Tell me about Ted. I remember your mentioning he lived close to you, so I suppose you witnessed some of the—"

"Yes, I . . ." Abby moistened her dry lips with the tip of her tongue. Then suddenly, as if she knew she had nothing more to lose, words began tumbling forth, and she found herself telling Joel about feelings she had never shared with anyone else. "One afternoon Ted and I were walking from my house to his, just the two of us—my grandparents tried very hard not to be too overprotective and let him live as normally as possible. And walking should have been a perfectly safe thing to do . . . except Ted was at that gangling, awkward age, twelve or thirteen, and he tripped over a clump of grass growing out over the sidewalk and fell, luckily, I thought, not on the concrete but into the grass. But there was a small sharp rock, and he cut his leg on it. It wasn't much of a cut, you know, but he knew, and I knew . . ." Abby squeezed her eyes shut and tried to still the tremors that suddenly rippled through her at the memory. "Oh, I was so scared, but Ted was, too; he went sort of pale, and I understand now why he must have. There he was alone with only a little kid like me to help him. I pretended to be calm and I put this makeshift pressure bandage on him, using his T-shirt, and after we propped his feet up on a hedge to elevate his legs, I ran to Grandma's house. But she had gone to the store, and I had to call the ambulance myself and ride to the hospital with Ted. I was so frightened, but I couldn't let him see I was, because Grandma had told me it always upset him even more to see everyone scared, but I still remember how terrifying it all was. . . ."

"Of course it was terrifying," Joel murmured soothingly, stroking her hair after the traumatic recollection had poured out in a rush of words. "An adult would be scared in a situation like that, and you were only a child. No wonder you were frightened; you had every right to be."

"I know that now. But then . . ." Abby breathed a tremulous sigh as she at last reopened troubled eyes to look up at Joel. "Then they all bragged about how brave I'd been. But I hadn't *felt* brave at all and I couldn't admit that, because I didn't want to disappoint them."

"My God, you learned to hide your feelings very early in life. I can understand now why you still hide them," Joel whispered, his dark gaze intensely tender as he laid his fingers against her cheek. "Is that why you haven't been able to tell me about the hemophilia? Because you thought you'd disappoint me?"

"Well, you are disappointed, aren't you?"

As Abby pressed her lips firmly together to stop their trembling, Joel shook his head. "You haven't disappointed me, Abby. I am sorry—"

"I don't want your pity, Joel," she said raspingly, sitting up straight only to have her shoulders caught by him before she could slip off the divan. She struggled a moment, then her useless efforts to escape ceased and she leaned her forehead against his arm, murmuring, "Feel anything besides pity, because I couldn't stand that."

"Hell, if I was to pity anybody right now, maybe it should be myself. At least you've known what was going on the past four months, while I thought you just didn't give a damn about me," he muttered roughly, encircling her slender neck with one hand, lifting her chin with his thumb to make her look at him. "I started to say I'm sorry you felt you couldn't tell me the truth about all this long before now. Did you really think I'd be disappointed in you, that it would matter—"

"But it does matter, Joel!"

"Of course it matters, but not enough to change my feelings for you. I love you so much, Abby," he whispered, kissing her eyebrows, her temples, and her lips. "I need you, and what you've just told me doesn't make me need you any less. And I still intend to marry you."

"Don't do this. It isn't fair to you or to me," she implored, twisting away from him to slip off the divan and walk across the room to the bed, where she wrapped her arms around one tall post and rested her head against it. Tears welled in her eyes but she blinked them back to meet Joel's gaze directly. She shook her head. "You know marriage wouldn't work for us. You want children so much, especially a son, and since I can't give you—"

"Ever heard of adoption, Abby?" Joel cut in rather impatiently, resting his elbows on his knees to watch her broodingly. "God knows, there are plenty of children in the world who need parents. And I've often thought I'd like to adopt one or two and be as much a father to them as I would be to my natural children." As Abby began to speak he lifted a silencing hand. "And don't say what you started to, because it isn't true. No matter what your mother thinks, no matter what you've come to believe, you *can* have children. *We* can have children. Granted, it wouldn't be quite as simple for us as for most other couples, but we'll have an advantage your parents didn't have: when you become pregnant, amniocentesis would tell us the sex of the fetus."

Abby's face paled; she looked close to tears. "Oh, Joel, I—I'm not at all sure I could ever choose to—abort your son. I'm not sure I could take a chance on giving birth to a daughter who might have to live with the reality of being a carrier, either. God, I'm not sure of anything."

"You don't have to be right now. I'm certainly not in

any great rush to have children. I think we'd want to be married three or four years at least before starting a family. And when we do decide we want children, we have options. Remember that, Abby," Joel said with quiet intensity, his gaze riveted on her as if he were trying to will the transference of some of his optimism into her. "You say you're not sure you could risk having a daughter who might be a carrier. Does that mean you wish your parents hadn't had you?"

"Well . . . no, I couldn't say that."

"Neither could I. I'm very glad they had you." A slight smile moved Joel's lips. "If you hadn't been born, Abby, I might never have known what it's like to love a woman the way I love you."

Abby's soft moan was nearly inaudible and she shook her head. "You're not playing fair when you say things like that. I need to think clearly, and you're appealing to my emotions."

"I'm simply telling you the truth. Now you tell me something. You said before that Ted *is* a hemophiliac, so it's obvious he's survived despite his affliction. What's his life like and his health?"

Abby gestured uncertainly, wondering why he asked these particular questions but, upon noting the adamant glint in his eyes, she answered. "Well, Ted will never be a robust person and he has problems with his joints, because past episodes of severe hemorrhage have damaged them. But he is involved in some new exercise program designed to help ease that complication; he says it helps." Abby paused, saw Joel's expectant expression, and continued. "Ted's married. And, of course, since even males afflicted with hemophilia aren't carriers, he and his wife have two children. He's an accountant."

"And would you say he wishes your grandparents had never had him?"

"No, he probably doesn't wish that, but—you have to

179

understand that he's a rather exceptional person. He tries so hard not to let anything get him down."

"And who's to say that if we had a son who was a hemophiliac, he wouldn't be an exceptional person, too. We could help him be, Abby," Joel said earnestly. "You're not sure you could ever abort a male fetus. Well, I'm trying to tell you we might well decide not to."

This was a possibility Abby had never been able seriously to consider, and her eyes widened and darkened with fear at the suggestion. "Maybe Ted is somewhat adjusted to his condition now but, my God, Joel, his childhood was a nightmare!"

"It sounds to me as if yours was, too."

"I never had to suffer like Ted."

"I think maybe you did. Not physically but emotionally. Abby, that one episode when you were a child and alone with Ted when he cut himself was enough to make you believe now that you simply cannot have children, that you don't dare risk it. But you're wrong. We do have options. We can have children, and you have to marry me, because I love you too much ever to let you leave me again."

What was left of Abby's composure dissolved then and there. She rushed across the room, sank down on her knees beside Joel, and, taking his hands, urgently brought them against her heart. Supplication was easily defined in her features as she looked up at him. "I love you too, and that's why you have to listen to me, please," she said, her voice quavering with emotion. "You say you love me too much to let me leave you, and I know you mean that . . . *now*. But what about in two years, or three or four? What if I could never risk having our own child? How would you feel then? I think you'd begin to resent me and I couldn't bear that. We'd both be hurt, so we have to end this now before that can happen to us."

"And if I can't convince you to change your mind, what

the hell am I supposed to do, Abby? Go out and find myself a brood mare who can give me a passel of children?" was Joel's strident and angry reply. "Do you think that would make me a happy man? Hell, no, it wouldn't, because I wouldn't have you, and you mean more to me than any baby ever could."

"But—"

"Be quiet," he demanded, his lean fingers now tangled in her hair yanking lightly to emphasize his command for silence. He looked down at her, exhibiting an intensity of emotion she had never witnessed in anyone before. A muscle ticked in his hard jaw. "Now you listen to me a minute. Suppose you weren't a carrier and we married, only to discover in two, three, or four years that I was sterile and we couldn't have children. Would you resent me, want to leave me to find some other man who could make you pregnant?"

"I know what you're leading up to, but—"

"Just answer the question," Joel persisted. "Would you leave me?"

"No! But—"

"Then how can you think *I'm* so shallow that I wouldn't want you anymore if you couldn't or wouldn't have my children, especially knowing the circumstances as I do?"

"Oh, Joel, I don't think you're shallow."

"You must, or you'd trust me enough to marry me. Why can't you simply say yes?"

"Because I'm just so scared," she admitted hoarsely as fat teardrops began to spill slowly down her cheeks. Her hands were uncertain, shaky, as they moved over his strong arms. "I do *want* to marry you, more than I've ever wanted anything, but I'm so very afraid that you might stop wanting *me* if I can't—"

"Don't be afraid, love. That'll never happen," he murmured, his smile infinitely gentle as he lifted her up onto his lap and gathered her close against him. His warm breath fanned her cheeks; his lips brushed over her tear-dampened skin before touching, then tenderly possessing, her yielding mouth. In silence, his hands reassured and comforted and caressed. He held her until her trembling stilled and she began slowly to relax in his secure embrace. His fingers coaxingly loosened the grip of her smaller ones, clutching his shirtfront. He lifted her hand and his mouth was firm and warm in the sensitized hollow of her palm as he softly said, "It's you I want, Abby, *you* I need."

Emitting a low heartfelt moan, she slipped her arms up onto his shoulders and laid her face against the side of his neck, unable to put up further resistance and no longer certain she even should make an attempt. It was as if she could physically feel Joel's love surrounding her and absorbing through the surface of her skin to sheath in warmth and peace the vital core of her being. Her words spoken against his smooth spice-scented skin were muffled when she finally said, "You have to be sure, Joel, very, very sure, you'll never stop loving me, because I—I don't think I could stand it if you did."

"I'll never stop," he promised, his breath stirring tendrils of her golden hair. "I tried to once and couldn't, and now I know I'll always love you."

"Even though I am defective?"

"I intend to teach you to stop thinking about yourself like that," he said, pulling back slightly to look down into her glimmering blue eyes. With the edge of one thumb he traced the curve of her cheek. "Abby, an abnormal chromosome doesn't make you any less perfect for me."

"You're sure?" she whispered back. "Absolutely?"

"*Absolutely.*" Joel smiled rather sheepishly. "And if you still have doubts about how much I love you, I can refer you to several scrub nurses, surgical teams, almost the entire medical center staff, who'll all tell you exactly what kind of hell it's been to work with me the last four months. I missed you so much."

"I missed you, too; it was such a horribly lonely time."

"It's over now, isn't it, Abby?"

"Yes. Oh, yes, it's over," she answered, convinced at last that a life shared with Joel had been predestined, that their futures lay ahead of them inseparably intertwined. Yet, a different uncertainty suddenly darkened her eyes as she gazed up at him. Her fingers played with one of his shirt buttons as she nibbled her lower lip for a second before allowing the question haunting her mind to tumble in words from her mouth. "I still don't know if I could ever risk having a son, Joel, considering what he might have to go through. Do you really think you could ever risk it?"

"I don't know," he answered honestly. "I do know that the quality of life for hemophiliacs has improved; they can lead fairly normal lives, since they can be treated in the home now with intravenous Factor Eight injections when needed."

"Unfortunately, those injections are so expensive."

"We should count ourselves lucky in that regard, then, shouldn't we?" Joel reminded her gently. "We could bear the expense, and you seem to be forgetting another advantage. I could teach you how to administer the injections. And, being a doctor, I'm nice to have around in the event of emergencies."

"You're nice to have around all the time," she told him. But her smile abruptly turned down as her lips trembled and cascading tears began. "Oh, Joel, it isn't fair. It isn't," she muttered, pressing her face against his chest.

It was an exorcism of a disappointment she'd never fully expressed, and Joel let her cry, saying nothing and only stroking her back while he held her in secure, loving arms until her sobs began subsiding. Then he ran his fingers through her hair and whispered against her right temple,

"You're right, Abby, it isn't fair. But there's something unfair in almost everyone's life, and I'm sure you realize that."

She nodded, then smiled tremulously while Joel used his handkerchief to dry her tears. "I thought I'd pretty much accepted being a carrier," she told him as he touched a corner of the folded white square to the one remaining teardrop imprisoned in the thick fringe of her lower lashes. "But when we met, and I started falling in love with you, then had to end everything because I was afraid to tell you the truth, acceptance became almost painfully impossible."

"And now?"

"Now I think I can deal with my feelings instead of hiding from them, because it makes all the difference that you can accept me despite the seriousness of my situation."

"*Our* situation. It'll be our situation from now on. And I don't just accept you; I welcome you, Abby," Joel said, deep and abiding love gentling his carved features while he looked down at her as if he never wanted to look away. "Soon after I met you, I began to realize that even with a busy practice and a fairly full social life, I was still lonely unless I was with you, so you're going to make all the difference in my life, too."

Tears brimmed in Abby's eyes again and spilled out, but this time she shed them in happiness, and they somehow accentuated the love that shone in the blue depths. Resting her head on Joel's shoulder, she laughed softly at herself. "I can't seem to quit crying, can I? I've done more of it lately than I usually do in two or three years."

"Then you're just making up for lost time," Joel said, ministering to her wet cheeks again with his handkerchief. He drew her close to him, kneading the muscles of her back, stroking her soothingly until every remnant of tension was banished and she was totally relaxed. But when she slipped one hand from his shoulder and her fingertips began to trace the subtle outline of the tendons in his neck, his own touch became less comforting and more sensuously caressing. His hands warmed her through the summer-weight fabric of her dress, yet she shivered as his lean fingers lingered in their exploration of her finely structured spine. He slowly feathered the surface of his nails from her tender-skinned nape down to her lower back. When his palm moved with gossamer lightness over her firmly rounded hips, Abby whispered his name as her lips sought his.

They exchanged slow tantalizing kisses as great drops of rain danced on the balcony beyond the opened French doors. A freshened breeze drifted into the room and over them as thunder rumbled in the distance. Abby lay in the circle of Joel's arms, her entire body tingling as the ball of his thumb played over her parted lips, brushing slowly back and forth again and again before slipping in between them, then beginning the breathtaking series of caresses once more. Her eyes watched his watching hers, and she was spellbound by the fervent passion and enduring love that were a steady flame in the once-mysterious dark depths.

She lifted a hand and touched his face. Her lightly skimming fingers followed the line of his strong jaw, then traveled in slowly drawn circles over his well-defined chin up to the very edge of his sensuously shaped lower lip. She felt the immediate acceleration of his heartbeat against her breast and shared a secret, intimate smile with him. She lazily rubbed the tip of her forefinger into the attractive faint indentations that creased his cheeks before teasingly touching first one corner of his mouth, then the other. With light strokes she traced the shape of his eyebrows and the straight bridge of his classically sculpted nose before sweeping her fingers little by little across the firm plane of his cheeks. A dreamy luminosity had softened her eyes to pools of dark blue as they looked deeply into his, and it was almost as if her tactile exploration of his features and his of her lips was hypnotizing both of them. As Abby trailed a finger across Joel's mouth he suddenly caught the tip between his teeth and gently nibbled, and feelings too deep and too complex ever to be completely analyzed or explained came to full flower within her.

"Joel, oh, I do love you," she breathed ardently.

"I love you, Abby," he told her, his deep voice gruff with emotion. "More than I can ever really say."

And the adoration that tempered the flaring glint of desire in his eyes provided Abby with one of those most precious moments in time that would be indelibly etched in her memory. Lost in his compelling gaze, she lay utterly pliant in his arms, his to do with as he pleased because she trusted him, and when he began undoing the buttons of her blue shirtwaist dress, her heart fluttered not with fear but with mounting excitement. With her belt unbuckled and the buttons unfastened, Joel soon deftly removed her dress, then tossed it onto the end of the divan. After slipping her slender feet out of her shoes, he sat her down on the divan, smiling at her when she intuitively stood with him.

Abby's pulses raced as he ran his fingers through her hair, allowing it to cascade down to drape a golden mantle around her lightly tanned shoulders. When he pushed the straps of her brief lacy bra down her arm, she reached out to start unbuttoning his shirt. Joel's hands moved around to unhook the bra, and before Abby had more than one of his buttons undone, he had freed her ivory, rose-tipped breasts to the rain-washed breeze that wafted over them and to his heavy-lidded gaze, which visually caressed. With the second shirt button, Abby's fingers fumbled tremblingly because Joel was now lowering both her half-slip and lacy panties. When his large hands reached her ankles, they exerted a light squeezing pressure that caused her to step out of those garments. In one slow, fluid motion, he raised himself, his palms scorching the backs of her bare legs as they followed an upward path over firmly molded buttocks to her delicate waist.

Joel, taking one short step back, lifted Abby's arms out from her sides, and his gaze, now burning hot, seemed to brand every inch of her glorious nakedness. Her smooth opalescent skin shimmered in the soft lamplight, and he simply looked at her, possessing her with his eyes. He released her hands but gently caught her arms and extended them out beside her again when she tried to let them drop.

"No, stay that way. And turn around for me, please. Very slowly," he instructed, his tone uneven. "Slowly, so I can really look at you."

As Abby pivoted gracefully before him she felt suddenly and unreasonably shy, her heart beginning to thud erratically, as if Joel had never before seen her like that. When she faced him once more and sensed he felt the same, she realized that in a very real way it was indeed their first time together. He knew everything about her then, and by telling him what she had believed she could never tell, she had made herself more vulnerable to him than she ever had been. Because she had done so, from that day forward their relationship would be even more poignantly intense, and the realization caused her breath to catch and brought an entrancing rose tint to her cheeks.

Noticing her heightened color, Joel smiled indulgently, perceptively, and extended his hands, taking hold of hers when she trustingly laid her fingers in his palms. "Come here, Abby," he said, drawing her to him. "Maybe you wouldn't feel quite as shy if you weren't alone in being undressed, and you know how to remedy that."

Much of Abby's shyness was burned away in the flames of desire that leaped higher and higher in her as she slowly removed Joel's clothing. His skin was burnished copper in the lamp's soft illumination, and by the time his magnificently male body was totally bared, she had to touch him. Her hands glided over his chest in slow circular motions, and he pulled her close against him, the fine hair on his muscular arms tickling her waist and causing sparks of fire to dance over her highly sensitized skin. For a long time they simply held each other, whispering their love until at last words alone were no longer enough for either of them. Their lips met and forged together. Joel's arms tightened around her as hers did around him. Abby's hot softly contoured flesh seemed to melt into his as his hands swept over her gracefully arched back. His stirring hardness pressed powerfully against her bare abdomen, and the emptiness within her clamored to be filled.

No words were necessary as they drew apart, and Abby rested her head against Joel's arm while they walked the short distance to the bed. When he had tossed back the coverlet, they sat down together on the edge but were immediately in each other's arms again, then lying together across the mattress. Abby's tender lips moved beneath his, her mouth opening wider, the tip of her tongue parrying, then submitting to the forceful invasion of his. Joel's hands were everywhere, playing over her full, throbbing hard-tipped breasts, her waist and hips, and intimately caressing every inch of her, heightening her passion so swiftly that her senses swirled dizzily. With more confidence than she had ever felt, she explored his taut body with a loving thoroughness that aroused his need of her to intolerability.

Abby's long smooth legs parted for him, her heart racing. Her breathing was ragged and her half-closed eyes were held by the glimmer of loving desire lighting the darkness of Joel's as, with a gently demanding thrust, he united his body with hers.

"Abby, Abby," he whispered, his hard lips playing lazily with hers. "I want you so much."

"And I love you so much," she whispered back. Entangling her fingers in his clean hair, she urged a rougher taking of her mouth.

With her secret no longer between them, they were swept up together into a lovemaking so tumultuous and poignantly enrapturing that they were bonded irrevocably, bodies and souls. Abby's passion rose rapidly to equal the finely honed edge of Joel's, and fulfillment's piercing ecstasy crested in wave after wave of such powerful sensations that he called her name aloud, and she cried out softly as pleasure and joyous warmth rushed within her.

Later, when their breathing and heartbeats were slowing to normal rates again, they lay close together in a tangle of warm damp limbs and tousled sheets, whispering sweet nothings that were everything into each other's ears. The kisses they exchanged were long and slow and lazy, while their caresses conveyed mutual wonder and more love than either of them had ever known.

"Abby," Joel murmured after a while. "We can get married tomorrow."

Her hand on his shoulder stroked his smooth skin and she nodded, though the lamp was out and he couldn't see her. "I'm ready, Joel."

"Umm, I think you're always *ready,*" he teased, then laughed softly at her when she retaliated by tickling him. "Tomorrow, then."

"Yes, tomorrow," she whispered. As the patter of the rain on the balcony and the soft steady sound of Joel's breathing filled her with real contentment, she touched her fingertips to his face. "You know, I was just thinking we will probably want to name our first daughter Faye."

Joel's facial muscles tensed slightly, then relaxed again. "And our first son, Abby? Will you want to name him David?"

"No." Her voice quavered on that word, then became strong and steady once more. "Well, maybe David could

189

be a middle name, but our son's first name has to be Joel. I insist."

Beneath Abby's fingertips, Joel's lips curved and formed a smile. She smiled back in the darkness, knowing that he knew that those few words she had just spoken had been the beginning of a hope he had brought to life in her. Her past had been too uncertain for her to be sure of the future, yet she did know beyond any doubt that she would share it with him, and that was what really mattered.

"I love you," she said softly, burying her face against his neck as he drew her closer against him. "I love you more than anything else in the world."

"And I love you. And, Abby," he added, smoothing her gloriously tangled hair, "you're all I'll ever really need. Remember that."

She would. She had a feeling he would never allow her to forget.

LOOK FOR NEXT MONTH'S
CANDLELIGHT ECSTASY ROMANCES ®